THE DRAGONPILLAR

By

Art Robertson

The Dragonpillar

© 2015 Art Robertson

Illustration by Darnell Dukes

Cover design by Sommer Stein

Copyedited by C.J. Pinard

For Ava, Brooklyn, Ellee, and Isabelle.

Before I became a grandparent myself, other grandparents would often tell me that even though your own children are special, grandchildren are that and so much more. Now I know what they were talking about.

yes!

TO: Bryn lee

With Love,
Grandma
&
Grandpa
Saunders

1-25-2016

Glossary of Terms

Albert Einstein: Famous German physicist who developed the theory of relativity. Most pictures of Einstein show him with very curly, wavy hair.

Apparition: Ghost, scary scene

Birdman of Alcatraz: Robert Franklin Stroud who spent 42 years in solitary confinement for murder. While in prison on Alcatraz Island in the San Francisco Bay, he studied birds and even published a relatively famous book entitled, *Diseases of Canaries,* hence the nickname, *Birdman of Alcatraz.*

Bovine: Scientific term used when referring to cattle.

Buck: Male deer.

Chagrin: Irritation, dislike.

CPR: Cardio Pulmonary Resuscitation (in the story it refers to Catch, Photograph, and Release).

Dilapidated: Old; worn out; rundown.

El Toro: Spanish for the word 'bull'.

Emanating: Beginning; starting.

Entomology: The study of insects.

GPA: Grade point average.

Hazmat: Hazardous materials.

Hoarder: Person who throws nothing away.

Home Economics: Class taught in school where students learn to cook and plan meals.

Inadvertently: Accidentally; not meaning to.

IU: Indiana University.

Reverse Engineering: Process of taking something apart piece by piece in reverse order it was constructed in order to see how it was built.

SUV: Sport Utility Vehicle.

Tetanus: Disease that causes lockjaw, a condition where a person cannot open their mouth.

The Titanic: 'Unsinkable' ocean liner that ran into an iceberg and sank on its maiden voyage, April 15, 1912, drowning 1,517 people.

TLC: Tender loving care.

UPS: United Parcel Service

Vet: Veterinarian. Doctor who treats animals.

Waiver: Hesitate. Change your mind.

Chapter 1
The Calm Before the Storm

Riding home from school, Ava was unusually quiet. Normally, all the girls would be talking and giggling, not only because it was Friday and her two cousins, Ellee and Isabelle, were staying for the weekend, but because Ava's birthday was tomorrow and a big party had been planned for that night.

Ava's mother, Jill, was one of the third grade teachers at her school. This meant that Ava, in the 5th grade, and her younger sister Brooklyn, in the 4th grade, did not have to ride the bus to or from school. They simply rode to school each morning with their mother, then rode back home with her each day when school was out.

Since their cousin Ellee was also in the 4th grade at the same school, she rode home with them each day as well, but not before Jill picked up her younger sister, Isabelle, at preschool. Ellee and Isabelle then stayed at Ava and Brooklyn's house until one of their parents picked them up after work, usually around five-thirty each evening.

But this weekend, Ellee and Isabelle were staying at Ava and Brooklyn's on one of their frequent sleepovers. This way they would already be there for Ava's birthday party the next night, but the girls also had something special planned for that morning, and it didn't have anything to do with Ava's birthday party.

On the way home, Jill noticed that three of the girls, Ava, Brooklyn, and Ellee, were unusually quiet, except for Isabelle. She was jabbering as usual, with a mouthful of candy from the 'exit bowl' at her preschool. Jill sensed that something was going on and decided to see if she could pry it out of them.

"How'd school go today, girls?" she asked, looking in the rearview mirror to see if her question triggered any unusual reactions.

"Fine," came the group's answer, as usual.

"You girls feel all right?" Jill asked, pressing further.

"Yes, we're okay," Ava answered, for all three.

"Well," Jill continued, "something happen at school today? You know you can always tell me."

1

"No, nothing happened at school today, mom, really," replied Ava.

Jill decided to let it drop. Whatever had clammed the girls up would eventually come out, she thought. And, if something had happened at school, surely she would have gotten a call about it. She decided to change the subject.

"Ava, everyone's coming to your party tomorrow night," she said.

Now, having been reminded of her party, Ava replied in a rather subdued tone, "Oh, I almost forgot. I can't wait. It'll be fun."

That's strange, Jill thought. Normally, the mention of a birthday party would get any group of young girls buzzing, but even this did not considerably change the atmosphere in the back of the car. Now Jill was sure something was up. But what?

Ava's mind was not on her birthday party. Still having to complete a project for her science class, she had enlisted her younger sister and her two younger cousins to help her with the project. As soon as they got to Ava's, they were going to finalize plans and make the necessary arrangements for tomorrow morning's hunt.

Ava, in her mind, kept going over and over the plan she had devised, weighing the consequences. If they got caught, they would be in a lot of trouble with their parents. If they were not careful, they could be seriously injured. And, it was possible that both these scenarios might play out, and she still would not find what she needed to complete her project. But Ava felt she had to take the risk, and when she had first presented her idea to the other three, they were all immediately on board.

Now, the closer they got to home, the more apprehensive Ava became. Suddenly the silence in the car was broken.

"Hey, what are these?" asked Brooklyn, reaching into the very back of their SUV.

Looking in the rearview mirror, Jill said, "Those are the two new butterfly nets your father promised he would make for you girls. Hopefully they will work better than that old, broken down one you've been using."

Brooklyn hauled one of the nets up over the backseat, and set in on her lap. The girls began examining how their father had constructed it. The contraption had a long, wooden handle with a sturdy wire loop firmly attached to one end. What looked like a sheer, nylon pillowcase was sewn onto the wire loop, creating a large opening where butterflies or insects could simply be scooped into the pillowcase. Then, by tilting the loop, the opening would close in on itself, thus trapping whatever was inside.

"Uncle Brett did a nice job on these," Ellee said.

"I wonder how my dad sewed that net on there?" wondered Ava.

"These should help a bunch!" exclaimed Brooklyn.

Yeah, Ava thought to herself, *Tomorrow morning they would need all the help they could get!*

"Thanks, mommy," Ava said.

"Don't thank me," Jill said. "Thank your father when he gets home."

"Okay, we will," said the girls.

Now, looking over at Brooklyn, Ava exclaimed, "Stop it, Brooklyn!"

Brooklyn was already attempting to dismantle the butterfly net they had been examining. Brooklyn had the annoying habit of taking things apart. Sometimes maybe just to see how things were made, or maybe just to see how they worked. But no one was really sure if those were her reasons or not. In any event, after an object had been dismantled, when put back together, the object usually did not resemble its original form nor did it work quite as well as it had prior to Brooklyn's reverse engineering.

"Brooklyn, stop it!" Ava exclaimed again. "There's not that much to it!"

Brooklyn stopped what she was doing, then began attempting to reattach the portion of the netting she had taken off the wire loop. By the time they arrived home, the butterfly net appeared to be back in its original, intended form.

However, leaning over, Ava whispered curtly to her sister, "That one's yours, Brooklyn," she said, pointing to the net she had just reassembled.

As their car pulled up to the farmhouse, Jill asked, "You girls going over to the meadow?"

Ava felt her heart start to race. "Uh... not today. We're going in the morning, if that's okay?" Ava asked.

"That's fine," Jill said, "as long as the weather is good. By the way, your father has to work in the morning." Now, turning around to look at Isabelle, she said, "I'm sorry, honey, but you won't be able to go with the girls in the morning."

Thinking Isabelle would start crying at hearing this news, Jill leaned over. Patting Isabelle on her shoulder she said, "Sorry, Izzy. We can bake some cookies while the girls are gone, and maybe when Uncle Brett gets home, he'll give you a ride around the farm on the Gator."

The girls started giggling. Jill couldn't figure out what she had said that was so funny, and was surprised to see that Isabelle was giggling as well, unfazed by the news that she wouldn't be going in the morning.

Ava spoke up, "Daddy already told us last weekend that he had to work tomorrow morning, so we went ahead and planned something for Isabelle to do."

Hmmm… I wonder what that could be? Jill thought to herself.

As they piled out of the car, Jill announced that they all had some chores to do before they started on anything else.

"In the laundry room," she said, "there are several loads of towels that need to be folded and a load in the washer that need to be taken out and put in the dryer, except for your father's tennis shoes. I washed them with the towels. They need to be taken out of the washer and set out on the back porch to air dry."

"Why can't we just throw them in the dryer with the towels?" asked Brooklyn. "It would dry them a lot faster."

"Because," Jill said, "the heat in the dryer will soften up the glue that holds the shoes together and they will fall apart. That's why."

"Cool!" exclaimed Brooklyn.

The other girls just rolled their eyes. The thought now occurred to Jill that Brooklyn might put the shoes in the dryer, just to see if they really would fall apart.

"Ava," Jill said, "why don't you unload the washer and take care of your father's shoes. The rest of you can fold the towels."

"Okay," they all agreed.

"Also," Jill added, "in the morning, before you go out, I want you all to make your beds and bring down your dirty clothes and put them in the laundry room."

"All right," they all said again.

When the girls got in the house, they finished their chores in record time and then disappeared upstairs.

"That's odd," Jill said out loud to herself. "No complaining about chores and no lollygagging around."

Jill went to check. All the towels were neatly folded and put away. The dryer had been reloaded with the wet towels, and the tennis shoes had been placed out on the porch to air dry, just as she had instructed. Still, Jill had the uneasy feeling that something was going on, but she couldn't put a finger on it yet. Jill noticed that even Snoop, the family dog, had disappeared. Usually, around this time of day, he would be patrolling the kitchen, looking for a handout as supper was being planned.

Chapter 2
Practice Makes Perfect

From the upstairs bedroom window, having previously studied the area to the north that was still fenced in, it appeared to Ava that this part of the meadow contained more wildflowers and plants than the rest, probably due to the fact that only one animal had been housed there, compared to the herd of cattle that had been trampling down the areas that she had already searched. She reasoned, then, that the odds of finding something she could use for her project would probably be much greater in there. When she ran this observation by the other girls, they all agreed.

Also, after Ava had learned that her father had to work this Saturday morning, her plan seemed to be coming together. Obviously, if one of the parents had been going along, the girls would not have been allowed to go into that area. But now, since her father had to work and no parent would be going along, they could explore that area of the meadow at will, as long as they could safely get over the barbed-wire fence, and as long as Mr. Gray's bull didn't suddenly show up. The only problem now was that since no adults would be going, that meant Isabelle would, once again, have to stay behind. For the moment, Isabelle was heartbroken, especially after hearing what the others were planning and the fact that she had still not convinced her parents to let her go to the meadow without adult supervision.

However, after learning that Isabelle had still not convinced her parents to let her go, the other three girls put their heads together, and in no time came up with what they thought was a brilliant idea. They decided to place Isabelle upstairs by the window that faced the meadow. While the other three were over there, Isabelle, with a pair of binoculars, could keep a constant lookout for danger, and with one of the two-way radios Ava had gotten out of her father's hunting pack, she could keep in constant contact with them in case she saw any trouble brewing.

When told about their plans for her, Isabelle loved the idea, and readily agreed. With her new duties, she felt she was now in charge of safety for the entire operation.

Now, upstairs in Ava and Brooklyn's bedroom, the girls crowded around Ava, going over the plan for tomorrow morning. They set up a table for Isabelle by the north window which overlooked the meadow. Ava got out some of her father's hunting gear that they would be using. Ava showed the other three girls how the equipment worked and had them practice with it until she was satisfied that each girl knew how to operate each item. Ava took extra time showing Isabelle how to adjust the focus on the binoculars and how to work the 'zoom-in' feature.

They all took turns looking out the window in the direction of the meadow, and were amazed at how much of the area they could see. They could even clearly see the shed, located up in the northernmost area, close to the woods.

"Is that where you guys are going?" asked Isabelle, referring to the area containing the shed.

Ava just solemnly nodded her head.

Next, Ava showed them how the radios worked; how to turn them on and how to adjust the volume and change the channels. Then Ava showed them the recharging unit plugged into the wall outlet and explained the importance of keeping the radios fully charged. "The radios should always be put back on the charger after being used," she said.

After learning how the radios worked, they had great fun talking back and forth, until the batteries finally gave out.

Putting them back on the recharging unit, Ellee asked, "What channel are we going to use?"

"Well," Ava said slowly, thinking. "My birthday's tomorrow, the 17th, so why don't we use channel 17?"

"Good idea," said Brooklyn. "Channel 17 it is."

Later that Friday afternoon, when Ava's father got home from work, he asked why his two-way radios were out. "Those are not toys, you know," he said to the group. The girls became quiet, thinking they might already be in trouble for leaving the radios out, or Ava's father may have already guessed what they were up to.

"We were just practicing," blurted out Brooklyn.

"Practicing for what"? Brett asked suspiciously. Ava was staring 'darts' at Brooklyn.

"Mmmm… well, you know," Ava stammered, "in case we have an emergency, we will know how to use them," she said unconvincingly.

Before their father had a chance to answer, Ellee cut in. "You know, Uncle Brett. If we were to go somewhere and say… say we forgot our cell phones. If we had these and knew how to use them, we might be able to radio for help." Smiling sweetly, she added, "It's like you always say. It's better to have and not need than to need and not have."

Having his own logic used against him by his nine-year-old niece caught him off guard. Ava's father had to pause and take a second to think about what to say next.

Hiding her face with a pillow, Ava almost burst out laughing. Surely her father was not going to fall for that line. Brooklyn, also quietly laughing behind her father's back, was giving Ellee a 'thumbs- up, nice one'.

"Well… er… okay," Brett stammered. "But when you're through practicing with them, make sure you put them back where you found them."

"Okay, daddy, we will," said Ava.

When Brett headed down the stairs, he mumbled to himself, "Those four girls! Where do they come up with this stuff?"

After supper, one by one, the girls disappeared back upstairs to the bedroom for one last rehearsal. Ava checked to make sure that Isabelle knew how to operate the binoculars and the two-way radios as, even though she was the youngest of the group, her part in the operation was probably the most critical to their safety. Ellee rechecked her backpack, making sure she had everything they might possibly need in the morning.

"Any questions?" Ava asked. "Anything we didn't go over?"

"Can't think of anything," said Brooklyn.

"Me neither," said Ellee.

Isabelle didn't reply. She was still busy practicing with the binoculars and her radio.

The only thing left to do now was wait until morning. Turning on the television, they checked the weather report. Tomorrow was going to be unusually warm, with a chance for showers later in the afternoon.

"We should have plenty of time," said Ava. "Weather's going to be perfect in the morning."

The Dragonpillar

The other three just nodded their heads in agreement. With nothing left to do, they decided to turn in early. After a little small talk, they all drifted off to sleep, Snoop on Ava's bed as usual, and the binoculars safely tucked away beneath the covers of Isabelle's bed. Before going to sleep, though, Ava suddenly remembered her birthday party. Having been consumed with preparations for tomorrow morning's mission, she again had completely forgotten about her party. She hoped that this time tomorrow night, she would be celebrating and having fun with family and friends, instead of worrying about her class project.

Chapter 3
The Dairy Farm

Two years earlier, in the spring of that year, the two families had gone in together to purchase the dairy farm from a Mr. Gray. He was a kindly old gentleman, now in his mid-eighties, and had wanted to retire from farming. As his children had grown up, they had taken jobs in other cities, not being interested in dairy farming. With no family to take over the operation of the farm, Mr. Gray now wanted to sell out and move closer to his children and grandchildren.

Ava and Brooklyn's parents, Brett and Jill, had for some time wanted to move out of the city limits, but to date, had not found what they were looking for. When they heard that this property had come up for sale, Brett immediately contacted his younger brother, Bryan, and his wife, Lee Ann, to see if they would be interested in the property as well. The property had lots of possibilities and perhaps both families could pool their resources to make the purchase.

Bryan called Brett and told him that they were indeed interested, as they also had been looking for property out of the city limits on which to build a new house. Brett then contacted the realtor handling the sale, and set up a day and time when both families could go and take a tour of the property. So, on the first available Saturday, they all piled into two vehicles and met the realtor, Mr. Sievers, at the farm.

The farm was located only three miles out of the city limits, so access to everything back in town would just be a short drive. The property consisted of eighty-two acres, divided into three separate tracts. The first tract included a two- story white clap-board farmhouse, sitting on seven acres. Behind the house was a huge cattle barn, and directly to the south of the barn was a three acre lake. There were also several small outbuildings scattered about the seven acres, including a couple of dilapidated chicken coops.

The second tract, north of the barn, consisted of forty-five acres of gently rolling meadow, where Mr. Gray's dairy cattle grazed. It was completely fenced in so the dairy cows would not be running loose on other people's property. The meadow gradually ran up hill from the south to the north, eventually butting up against a hilly, wooded area.

The Dragonpillar

Of this wooded area, Mr. Gray owned thirty acres of timber, which was also included in the sale along with the other two tracts of land. Three acres of this wooded area, along with three acres of the adjoining meadow, were fenced in separately from the rest of the meadow by a barbed-wire fence. This was the area where Mr. Gray kept his prize 1200 lb. bull. Also located in this area, close to the wood-line, was an outbuilding which not only contained a stall for the bull to sleep in, but doubled as a tool shed as well.

Emanating somewhere out of the wooded hills to the north was a slow moving creek, which ran slightly downhill to the south, winding its way through the entire length of the meadow. The creek was fed by a warm spring. In the winter, parts of the creek near its source never froze over due to the constant supply of warm water. Along its length, the creek was dotted with small, shallow pools where Mr. Gray's cattle would cool off on hot summer days. In these pools, small fish fed on the unfortunate insects that would fall off the greenery growing along its banks. Eventually, the creek wound its way down behind the barn, then emptied into the small lake behind the farmhouse. As the water level in the lake was constantly on the rise due to being spring-fed, the water would spill over and down the opposite bank, the creek then continuing on to the south, through other various farms and fields.

After touring the property with Mr. Gray and Mr. Sievers, both sets of parents knew this would be the perfect place to raise their families; that is, if it could be bought for the right price.

The farmhouse had been well maintained and had much more room that Brett and Jill's current house. There was even enough room that Ava and Brooklyn could each have their own separate bedrooms, or the upstairs could be turned into one giant bedroom, which would be perfect when their cousins Ellee and Isabelle would come for weekend sleepovers. Of course, when the bedroom options were presented to Ava and Brooklyn, the upstairs bedroom was the only choice.

The huge cattle barn, now empty, would not only serve as a workshop and storage area, but would also serve as a neat place to hold parties and family get-togethers. The girls, however, had other ideas regarding the barn: a giant playhouse, they all envisioned, rubbing their hands together in excited anticipation.

As for the meadow, Bryan and Lee Ann would now have the perfect place to build their new house. After their new house was built, they would never have to make a lengthy trip during the school year to pick up Ellee and Isabelle after work. They could now simply drive home, walk over the short distance to Brett and Jill's, and walk back to their house with their girls.

"Easy-peasy, lemon-squeezy," Ava had said to everyone upon hearing the parents discussing this advantage. They all laughed.

As for the three acre lake, everyone in both families liked to fish, except for Jill and Lee Ann, and now they would have a convenient place to wet a line. Brett and Bryan would even have thirty acres of woods to hunt in, if the girls would let them.

When the tour of the property was finished, they all shook hands with Mr. Gray and thanked him for his hospitality. The parents told him they were really interested in purchasing the property, however they wanted to go home and 'crunch' the numbers to see if they could afford it. Hopefully, they told Mr. Gray, they would be able to make him an offer in a few days. Before they left, Mr. Gray gave each family a jar of honey he had personally collected from his own beehives.

In less than a week, the two families made Mr. Gray an offer on his property. He thought their offer was more than fair, and accepted it without even bothering to make a counter offer, much to the chagrin of his realtor. The adults all shook hands on the deal, and before the parents left to go work out the details, the girls headed to the barn to check out their new giant 'playhouse'.

Gesturing toward the girls, Mr. Gray said, "I think they're going to like it here."

"We're all going to like it here," said Lee Ann wistfully.

"It's perfect!" exclaimed Jill, thinking of all the possibilities the property offered.

As the details were laid out, Brett and Jill would pay for the seven acre tract containing the house, barn and outbuildings, and the three acre lake. The remaining two tracts would then be evenly split between the two families. The plan was, after Bryan and Lee Ann had decided where to locate their new house, they would then divide the remaining acreage of the meadow into building lots and, at some point in the future, sell the lots off to help pay expenses when and if the girls decided to go to college.

Once the purchase was complete, it didn't take long for Mr. Gray to round up and sell off his livestock, especially since Brett and Bryan helped with the 'cattle drive'. In appreciation for their help, Mr. Gray helped Brett and Bryan take down most of the fence around the lower part of the meadow near the house and barn. However, the areas further to the north, they left for later.

The Dragonpillar

By the time Brett and Jill moved in that first spring, all the animals were gone, except for a few 'escapees' from the chicken coop, running around loose in the yard. The flowers and foliage in the meadow, now, not being trampled or eaten by the dairy cows, emerged with a vengeance.

Ava, Brooklyn, and Ellee were told they could go exploring in the meadow as long as the weather was nice, and they told their parents when they were leaving and how long they thought they would be gone. And of course, they were told to stay out of that part of the meadow that was still fenced in.

Isabelle, on the other hand, being only two and a half years old at the time, was not allowed to go unless one of the parents accompanied her. Being rather strong-willed, this did not set too well with her. However, much to her credit, she did not cry about it. Most of the time, she simply found something else to do around the house, until her sister and two older cousins returned.

Chapter 4
The Green and Yellow Alligator

Shortly after moving in, Ava's father, Brett, purchased a used four-wheel all-terrain utility vehicle to help with chores around the farm. He also purchased a matching flatbed trailer, which could quickly and easily be attached to the back of the four-wheeler. He said the trailer would make hauling items around the farm much easier, and that proved to be right.

On some weekends, when the weather was nice, Brett would hook the trailer up and give all the girls, including Snoop, a ride around the farm and up through the meadow. On these trips, Isabelle was allowed to ride along.

Riding around the farm was great fun, and the girls got to see a lot of interesting things they would not have otherwise had the opportunity to see in town. However, there was one thing the girls just couldn't figure out, and it concerned the four-wheeler they were riding on.

All the adults call the vehicle a 'Gator'. Yeah, the girls could see it was sort of an alligator-green color all right, but to the girls, it didn't look much like an alligator. Also, to make it more confusing, bright yellow letters were painted on both sides of the engine compartment, clearly identifying it as some kind of a deer. A John Deere, to be exact. And even more obvious was the bright yellow silhouette of a leaping buck painted on the front above the grill. To the girls however, the four-wheeler didn't look much like a deer either, but that's what it said.

Needless to say, the girls couldn't figure out how their parents could confuse the vehicle with an alligator, or much less, how their parents could miss the bright yellow lettering, making a proper identification of the vehicle so obvious. However, after much deliberation, the girls decided not to point out their parents' continual mistake. They thought that in doing so, it might prove to be somewhat embarrassing for the adults, which then, the girls figured, might translate into fewer rides on the four-wheeler. So the girls just kept quiet and went with it.

From then on, every time the girls got to ride on the vehicle and one of their parents would mention the word 'Gator', the girls would look at each other and start giggling. To this day, their parents never figured out the real reason why the girls were always laughing and giggling when the word 'Gator' was mentioned.

The Dragonpillar

On the very first trip riding through the meadow, Brett warned all the girls, "I know you girls all know how to swim, but stay out of that creek. Even though it isn't very deep, while Bryan and I were helping Mr. Gray round up his cattle, we found out that its bottom is nothing but sticky, mucky clay. If you wade in there, you'll get stuck, and then you will have to call someone to come and pull you out!"

Nearing the section to the north that was still fenced in with barbed-wire, he added, "And don't go climbing this barbed-wire fence either. You will not only get cut up, but you will probably then have to get a tetanus shot as well."

To make a really lasting impression on the girls, he also added, "You see that shed up there, close to the woods?" Looking in that direction, the girls all nodded. "That's where Mr. Gray kept his prize 1200 pound bull! Before we moved in, while Bryan and I were helping him round up his dairy cows, Mr. Gray said it would be a good idea if we didn't go in there. He said that bull had gotten so mean, it would be better if we just left it alone, which we did. Mr. Gray said he would wait until he was able to get a lot more help before trying to corral it and load it up in his truck. As far as I know, Mr. Gray hasn't been back, so that bull's probably still running around in there somewhere. If you cross over that fence and that bull shows up, he will probably trample you flat, or worse!"

The girls all looked again in the direction of the shed, this time with real terror on their faces. They had all heard the stories at school about that bull injuring some high school students a few years back. Wide-eyed, they all agreed it would be a bad idea to climb that fence. They all promised never to go.

In the two years that had passed, the girls had heeded their father's warnings about the fence. But now circumstances had changed, and sometimes promises are made to be broken.

Ava and Brooklyn rationalized that it had been nearly two years since that first trip on the Gator, when their father had warned them about the bull, and in all that time while living on the farm, they had never seen a cow, much less a bull, anywhere on the property. However, as it were, things were about to get more complicated.

15

Chapter 5
Bobby

That night Ava lay awake staring at the bottom of the bunk above her. She was not able to sleep, still going over in her mind all their preparations and worrying about what might go wrong in the morning. Suddenly a voice from above broke her train of thought and the silence in the room.

"Ava," whispered Brooklyn, "have you seen my bobby?" she asked.

"No. I haven't seen it. Did you check downstairs?" Ava whispered back.

Brooklyn climbed down the ladder from the top bunk and, going over to her dresser, turned on the lamp. After quietly searching the room, she wailed, "I can't find my bobby!"

"Shh… " Ava warned. "You're gonna wake up Ellee and Isabelle!"

"I need my bobby!" Brooklyn wailed again as she headed down the stairs to search for her blanket.

The girls had already been in bed for some time. Brett and Jill were in the kitchen, making small talk about the farm over cups of coffee, when Brett heard a noise. Looking into the living room he said, "What are you doing up?"

"I'm looking for my bobby!" Brooklyn cried once more.

Trying not to yell too loud, Jill said, "It's in the dryer. I washed it today when we got home, after you girls finished the towels. I just forgot to tell you."

Brooklyn padded off to the laundry room, opened the dryer door, and retrieved the pink and yellow blanket, covered in quarter-sized brown and white polka dots. After a quick inspection, satisfied that bobby had not been harmed by the dryer, she padded back upstairs with her blanket, climbed the small wooden ladder, and crawled back into bed without further fuss.

With Ava, now nearly asleep, she once again heard a voice coming from the top bunk. Opening her eyes, she stared at the bedsprings above her and waited.

"Ava, you still awake?" Brooklyn whispered again.

The Dragonpillar

"I am now," Ava said, mildly perturbed at being disturbed again. "What is it this time, Brooklyn? Didn't you find bobby?" she asked.

Ignoring the question, Brooklyn asked, "Ava, you still have your bobby?"

"I never had a bobby. I had a blankey," Ava responded.

"But do you still have it?" pressed Brooklyn.

"I have mine," spoke a voice from one of the twin beds close by. Ellee.

"I have mine, too," spoke another voice from the other twin bed. Isabelle.

Great! thought Ava. *Now everyone's awake!*

Brooklyn heard Ava slide out of bed, her feet softly hitting the floor. She went over to her dresser and turned on the lamp. The other three girls watched as she pulled out the bottom drawer, searching through the clothes. Somewhere, from the very back of the drawer, she tenderly pulled out a small, neatly folded blanket. Holding it up to her cheek, its familiar softness immediately brought back a flood of fond memories.

"Yeah, I still have it," Ava said, pausing briefly, as if torn by what to do next. Reluctantly, she carefully refolded the little blanket and placed it back into the drawer. Slowly closing the drawer, she turned off the light and slid back into bed, at the same time quietly scolding Snoop, who had taken advantage of her short absence, to hog even more of the covers.

"It's like having a fifty pound hairy bowling ball lying across your ankles!" she said to the dog, as she attempted to scoot him over. Even with this admission, the other three girls were somewhat jealous. Snoop always slept on Ava's bed.

As Ava got situated, Brooklyn looked down and whispered one more time. Frustrated, Ava said, "What is it this time?"

"Ava, how did you know when it was time to stop using your blankey?" she asked timidly.

Even in the dark, Ava could sense that this question had piqued the interest of her two younger cousins, as they had rolled over on their sides to listen intently to her answer. Ava thought for a moment before answering, knowing her answer would have an impact on the other three. She chose her words carefully.

"I guess as you get older you just become more involved in school and other things like sports, and hobbies, and such. When that happens and there is so much to do, it seems like the time just flies by. Then one

17

day, you realize that your blanket, for some reason, has disappeared and you didn't even notice. At that point, I guess you figure that you really don't need it anymore, and you just sort of forget about it from then on. It's something like that."

The other three girls were quiet for a moment, and Ava hoped that her answer made some sense to them.

"Well," Brooklyn finally said, "how old were you when that happened?"

"Mmmm… " thought Ava. "I'd say I was probably about your age. Why?"

"Oh, I don't know," said Brooklyn. "Just wondering."

With the girls mulling over what Ava had said, the room became quiet once again. Unexpectedly, a voice from one of the twin beds asked, "Ava, does Snoop have a blankey?"

"No, Isabelle, Snoop doesn't have a blankey," Ava laughed, scratching Snoop's ears. "Now everyone go to sleep. We have a big day tomorrow."

Little did Ava know how prophetic her words would become.

Chapter 6
Good Things Come in Small Packages

The next morning the girls awoke to a beautiful spring morning in Indiana. The sun was up and there wasn't a cloud in the sky. A mild breeze was coming out of the southwest.

The girls quickly finished up their morning chores, making their beds and taking their dirty clothes down to the laundry room. As they quickly ate breakfast, Jill noticed the usual small talk around the breakfast table was being kept to a minimum.

As the girls were finishing up breakfast, Jill said, "Ava, I think the UPS man stopped out front this morning. I bet he left a package on the front porch. You think you should go see what it is?" She thought it was probably a birthday present from someone who could not attend her party that night.

Ava pushed away from the table, followed by the other girls, and went to look. Finding a package on the front porch, just as her mother had said, she picked it up and carried it into the kitchen, setting it on the table.

"I wonder what it could be," Ava said.

Examining the box, they noticed a handwritten message on the top. The message read: *Ava, open immediately upon arrival.*

"Can I open it?" Ava asked her mother.

"Well," Jill replied, "it's probably a birthday present. Don't you want to wait until tonight?" The girls just stared at the box. "Well, it does say to open it immediately, so, I guess it's up to you," her mother said.

Ava tore into the box. With the other three girls crowded around, she reached down into the outer box and pulled out a smaller shoebox. Removing the lid, Ava exclaimed, "Wow! Look! It's those really cool tennis shoes I showed Mamaw online!"

Ava hurriedly put the shoes on. They fit perfectly. "Wow, they're awesome!" she exclaimed again, modeling the shoes for the now slightly jealous spectators.

"Ava, there's a card in there," Jill pointed out.

Ava reached into the box, producing an envelope. Opening it, she read it aloud: "Ava, hope these arrive before your party. Happy Birthday! Mamaw and Papaw."

"You will have to call and let them know you got them," Jill said. "And be sure to thank them," she added.

"Okay, I will," said Ava.

The girls began putting the dishes in the sink and finished cleaning off the kitchen table. Then, they quickly headed upstairs to round up their equipment for the morning hunt, including their two new butterfly nets and Ava's plastic collection jar. Isabelle stationed herself at the table by the window while the other three girls hurriedly ran back down the stairs.

Hearing them, Jill yelled, "Ava, be sure to take your new shoes off!"

"Okay, mommy," Ava yelled back, still in a big hurry and not really concentrating on much of anything other than getting out of the house and over to the meadow.

Hearing the girls running down the stairs and hurrying through the house, Jill yelled, "You girls leaving now?"

"Yes," they all yelled back at the same time.

"Where's Isabelle?" Jill hollered

"She's upstairs, drawing," Ava yelled back.

"Uh... okay. You girls have your cell phones?" Jill yelled again.

"Got'em," came the hasty reply.

"Okay, good," said Jill. "Make sure you're back by at least three p.m. Your party starts at six and I need you girls to help me get some things ready before people start showing up."

With that, Jill heard the screen door open wide as the girls went out the front door. Jill instantly yelled, "Don't slam the screen door!"

Whack! Too late.

Suddenly Jill realized that even when she herself went out either the front or back screen door, no matter how careful she was, the door always seemed to slam shut on her as well. She laughed.

"I guess it's really no big deal," she thought to herself. "In fact, I'm growing rather fond of that sound."

"There's nothing like living on a farm. Roosters crowing in the morning and screen doors slamming all day long. Does it really get any better than this? I guess living in the city you just seem to forget about some of the simpler pleasures in life," she said, as she smiled to herself.

Sighing, she went back to working on her lasagna for that night's dinner party. She slid the lasagna into the oven, leaving the oven light on so she could watch its progress as it baked.

"Already smells good, doesn't it, Snoop?" Jill asked the dog.

Staring at the lasagna through the glass panel in the oven door, Snoop approvingly sniffed the air and wagged his tail. Looking at the dog, Jill swore she could see the wheels turning in his head.

Just then, Jill heard the front screen door open back up. "Come on, Snoop!" Ava yelled.

"Go on, Snoop," Jill urged. "The girls are waiting for you."

Glancing one last time through the oven door at his prize, Snoop grudgingly turned and headed toward the front door.

With that, Jill heard the tension on screen door spring start to increase as Ava held the door wide open for Snoop to go through.

Without thinking, Jill yelled again, "Don't slam the screen door!"

Whack! Too late. The screen door banged shut once again.

Old habits are hard to break. Apparently, new ones as well.

After Ava, Brooklyn, Ellee, and Snoop went out the front door, Jill went to check on Isabelle. Just to make sure Isabelle was where she was supposed to be, Jill quietly crept up the stairs, peeking into the girls' bedroom. Sure enough, Isabelle was sitting at a table under the north-facing window, with her drawing materials and a few other miscellaneous items.

Jill knocked on the door. "You okay, Isabelle?" she asked.

Slightly startled, Isabelle replied, "Uh… yeah, I'm okay, Aunt Jill."

"You need anything, maybe something to drink?" Jill asked.

"No," Isabelle replied, as she attempted to coax another sip out of a partially frozen bottle of water. "Ellee gave me this," Isabelle said, holding up the bottle of water for Jill to see.

"Well, if you need anything else, just let me know," Jill said.

"Okay, thanks, Aunt Jill," Isabelle replied.

As Jill started down the stairs, she turned and added, "I'm sorry you didn't get to go with the other girls this morning, but they probably won't be gone that long."

Gazing out the window, Isabelle replied in a worried tone, "Yeah, I hope not."

"You want to help me bake Ava's birthday cake later on?" Jill asked.

"Yeah, but I'm gonna stay up here and draw for now," she replied, not taking her eyes away from the window.

Satisfied that things were as they should be, Jill went back downstairs to check on her lasagna. Besides the colored pencils, crayons, drawing paper, and Isabelle's GI Joe doll, she either didn't notice or failed to comprehend the meaning of the unusual drawing instruments sitting on Isabelle's table: a pair of high-powered binoculars and a fully charged two-way radio.

Chapter 7
The Lookout

Sitting alone at her drawing table, strategically placed by the second floor window of Ava and Brooklyn's bedroom, Isabelle gazed out the window to the north. She had a complete view of the entire meadow from this vantage point. Resting on the table were her drawing pencils, a pencil sharpener, sheets of drawing paper, crayons, a large box of colored pencils, and of course the 'other' items her Aunt Jill had failed to notice.

Isabelle loved to draw, and nearly five years old, she was fairly accomplished at sketching things out from memory. Even though she had made limited trips around the farm with the other girls and her Uncle Brett, she still had many new ideas to put to paper.

Each day after preschool, she would come home with an armload of new drawings which would immediately replace the ones stuck all over the refrigerator from the previous day. Everyone agreed that she was quite artistic for a four-year-old. *Almost five*, she would remind them.

Isabelle had waited a long time to be included in one of the older girls' adventures. They had assigned her some very important duties and they were counting on her. But now, gazing out the window, lost in thought, she was absentmindedly twisting her long, strawberry blonde hair.

Last weekend, Isabelle learned what the other three girls were planning for this morning and she knew she probably wouldn't get to go.

Isabelle had again tried to reason with her parents that she was old enough to go exploring in the meadow with the other girls without an adult going along, but her parents still said 'no.' They told her that she had to be at least six before she could go unaccompanied by an adult. Since her birthday was coming up in late June, when she would turn five, she figured that she only had to wait a little over a year. However, for now, she decided to try a different approach.

She reminded her parents that Snoop, Ava and Brooklyn's dog, always went along on these trips. Isabelle reasoned then, that since Snoop was eleven years old, in human years that would make him seventy-seven years old. She told her parents that that should qualify as more than enough adult supervision.

When this argument was put to her parents, Bryan and Lee Ann tried not to laugh, not wanting to add insult to injury. However, her parents did not buy the 'Snoop' argument either. Instead, they congratulated her on a 'nice try', telling her they could see the logic in her reasoning, but the answer was still 'no.'

After Isabelle had given up and left the room, Bryan and Lee Ann had a good chuckle. "The other girls must have helped her with that one!" Bryan said.

"Yeah," said Lee Ann. "That was pretty well delivered for a preschooler, though. I wonder what she'll try next?"

"Really!" Bryan said. "When those four get together, who knows what they're going to come up with next!"

Little did their parents know what *was* coming up next.

Suddenly, Isabelle was startled by a noise, bringing her out of her thoughts and back to the task at hand. It was the sound of the back screen door slamming shut. Isabelle looked down and saw her sister, two cousins, and Snoop preparing to leave. Isabelle heard her radio pop.

"Isabelle, you there? Over."

Fumbling with the radio, finally Isabelle replied, "I'm here, Ava."

The other girls had now advanced past the barn and chicken coops and were about to start into the meadow.

"Isabelle, we're counting on you," said Ava. "I'll give you a shout when we reach the barbed-wire fence. At that point you need to keep a really sharp eye out, over."

"Okay," responded Isabelle. Looking through the binoculars she added, "I see you guys. Good luck and be careful. You can count on me."

"Thanks Isabelle. Over and out," said Ava.

"Command Post Isabelle in operation," added Isabelle proudly, in her best 'official' sounding tone.

"Command Post Isabelle?" questioned Ava, laughing.

"She watches a lot of GI Joe cartoons and our neighbor is in the Army" said Ellee, laughing as well.

"Uh-oh!" Ava said.

"What?" the other two girls asked.

"When Izzy was talking the last time, I heard cartoons on in the background, and it sounded like GI Joe!"

"Do you think she'll stick with us the whole time?" Brooklyn asked Ellee.

"Who knows," replied Ellee. "We'll find out soon enough."

"We should have unplugged the TV," Ava said matter-of-factly.

Chapter 8
I Don't Need to Go and See the Wizard

The girls headed into the meadow with anticipation. They were fairly familiar with the terrain in this section of the meadow, as they had been there numerous times, whether by walking or by riding around on the Gator with their parents. However, they still kept the conversation to a minimum and their eyes open, in hopes of spotting an insect that Ava could use.

Continually heading in a northerly direction, they diligently examined each patch and clump of flowers they came to, but nothing unusual presented itself. Even Snoop seemed to be caught up in the search, as he would sniff around the bushes and patches of foliage before disappearing into the greenery.

"Maybe Snoop will jump a rabbit," Brooklyn said.

"Do you think your dog can actually run down a rabbit?" Ellee asked.

"Not a chance!" Ava said laughing. "The rabbits sit around in the yard back at the house and just laugh at him."

"Poor Snoop," consoled Brooklyn, petting the dog's head and scratching his ears. "Don't listen to them, Snoop. I believe in you." Snoop sat down, looking somewhat dejected.

"I think he heard that," Ellee said to Ava, pointing to the dog's reaction. The girls all bent down to scratch Snoop's head in an attempt to build his confidence back up. "It's all right, Snoop, we understand," all the girls now said while making over the dog.

In Snoop's mind the insults weren't so bad. He had learned to work the girls for sympathy, which usually then translated into forthcoming doggy treats. Now his interest seemed to be magically renewed as he got up and began wagging his tail.

"See," said Ellee. "Your dog just needed a little T.L.C. It's already done wonders for him."

"I'm not sure that's the 'T.L.C.' he had in mind," said Ava. "It would be more like, Treats, Leftovers, and Chocolate!" They all laughed.

As they continued on, the girls eventually came upon the area that was sectioned off with the barbed-wire fence. Ellee took off her heavy backpack and set it on the ground. Ava produced a small pair of folding binoculars she had tucked away in her back pocket, and began scanning the area on the other side of the fence, looking not only for a more promising place to search, but for danger as well.

"Looks even better than what we saw from the window," Ava said approvingly.

Taking a turn with the binoculars, Ellee said, "Yeah, there are way more flowers in there, especially over there along the creek. Standing here at ground level though, makes it harder to see very far in," she added.

Upon hearing this, Brooklyn became more apprehensive, beginning to worry about what might be able to sneak up on them once they were on the other side.

Without saying anything, Ellee began slowly walking down the fencerow, carefully examining each section of fence, apparently searching for something.

"Better check in with Isabelle," Ava said. With Brooklyn nervously standing by her side, Ava held up the radio and pressed the 'transmit' button. "Isabelle, come in, over."

"I'm here, Ava," came the reply from the house.

"Do you see anything? Over," Ava asked again.

From the other end, Isabelle replied, "I don't see nothing, Ava."

Turning to her sister, Ava asked, "What do you think?"

"Let's go. I want to go in, I do," replied Brooklyn, much to Ava's surprise. Ava felt sure that when they got to this spot, her sister would back out, but apparently she was wrong.

"But how are we gonna get over the fence, Ava?" Brooklyn asked.

Ava was about to answer, when Ellee, who was standing further down the fencerow, spoke up, "Hey, you guys, come here and look at this."

Ava and Brooklyn walked down to where Ellee was standing.

"Look," Ellee said, pointing.

"What is it?" asked Brooklyn.

"A gate," responded Ellee proudly, "grown over with weeds and vines."

"How did you know there was a gate down here?" asked Ava.

"I didn't," said Ellee, "but I figured if Mr. Gray kept livestock in here, at some point he would have had to either get them in or get them out, so that meant that there had to be a gate somewhere."

Ava gave Ellee 'knuckles'. "Good job, Ellee."

"Maybe we can open it," Brooklyn offered.

"I doubt it," said Ellee. "See that chain? It's wrapped around the gate and fence post, and it's padlocked," she said.

"But we can clean some of the vines off and climb over it!" Ava said excitedly.

"That's right," said Ellee.

Ava and Ellee started pulling the vines off while Brooklyn walked back down the fencerow to retrieve their butterfly nets, Ava's collection jar, and Ellee's backpack.

Returning to the gate, Brooklyn set the equipment down. "Your backpack is pretty heavy!" she said.

Ellee simply ignored the comment.

As they prepared to climb over the gate, Ava reminded them, "From here on out, we need to keep the noise down. No need to announce our presence." The other two solemnly nodded their heads, understanding what Ava was referring to.

Brooklyn quietly slid the butterfly nets and jar under the fence, while Ellee struggled to get her backpack under the prickly wire.

"You could just leave that over here and pick it up when we come back," Ava said.

Ellee caught her two cousins looking dubiously at her backpack. They had no idea what was in it, but judging from its bulging sides, they were sure it was not only full, but heavy, as Brooklyn had just found out.

"Well," Ellee whispered, looking at her backpack, "you never know when some of this stuff might come in handy."

Uh-oh, thought Ava. "*Here it comes.*"

"Daddy says it's better to have and not need, than to need and not have," said Ellee.

The other two girls just rolled their eyes. They had heard Papaw say this numerous times, and now, besides their father, apparently Ellee and Isabelle's father had picked up on the phrase as well.

Ava thought to herself, *Ellee's usually pretty resourceful, so if she wants to lug that thing around, who am I to complain? Besides, it is hard to argue with her logic.*

"One thing to remember," Ava whispered to Ellee. "Once we get over the fence, in the event that we have to run for it, you might have to ditch that backpack."

"Let's hope it doesn't come to that," Ellee whispered back.

Ellee didn't want to think about ditching her precious pink backpack. She took it with her everywhere she went, but she knew Ava was right.

Ava took a deep breath and whispered, "Well, here goes nothing." To her surprise, she easily climbed up and over the gate, followed by Ellee, then Brooklyn. As soon as their feet landed in the soft grass on the other side, Ava was on the radio.

"Isabelle, what does it look like now? Over," asked Ava.

Scanning this area of the meadow, Isabelle replied, "Looks okay. I still don't see nothing."

"Roger that. Over and out," replied Ava, pocketing the radio.

Having finally succeeded in squeezing her backpack under the fence, once on the other side, Ellee picked it up and once slung it over her shoulder, giving Ava a thumbs-up at the same time.

Picking up the collection jar and their butterfly nets and handing one to Ava, Brooklyn asked, "Now what? Which way do we go?"

Quickly scanning the area herself, Ava whispered. "The stream leads up that way," she said, pointing to the north. "I say for now we just stick close to the bank and see where it leads us."

Ava, noticing that Brooklyn was starting to waiver, looked at her sister and asked, "What?"

"Ava," Brooklyn whispered, "ask Isabelle if anything is moving up there around that shed."

Glancing in that direction, Ava pulled the radio back out of her pocket and once again radioed the house. "Isabelle," she said, "can you see the shed? Over."

"The little house?" replied Isabelle.

"Yes, the little house. Anything moving around up there? Over," Ava asked again.

Scanning the area one more time, Isabelle replied, "No, nothing moving, except a few squirrels in that big tree."

"Okay, thanks, Isabelle. I'll check in with you every twenty minutes or so, but if you see anything at all, call us immediately, over."

"Okay, Ava, I will," came the reply.

At this point, there was nothing left to say. They simply lined up and marched off, with Ava in the lead, followed by Ellee, and Brooklyn bringing up the rear.

With the most dangerous part of their mission now underway, what seemed like such a good idea to Ava at the time, when she had carefully devised her plan in the safety and comfort of their bedroom, didn't seem like such a good idea to her now.

Nevertheless, the warmth of the mid-morning spring sunshine, the smell of fresh flowers in bloom, and the promise of new discoveries, somehow steeled her resolve. She pushed on to the north, following the stream, with the others in tow.

Chapter 9
Manna from Heaven

"Come on," Ava whispered, motioning to the other two girls as they fell into line. Ava kept her eyes forward, keeping up a constant vigil in the direction they were moving as the creek led them farther and farther away from the farmhouse.

"So far, so good," said Brooklyn, trying to sound more confident than she actually felt.

Holding her index finger to her lips, Ava again reminded them to keep their voices down, as she looked mostly at her sister. Brooklyn and Ellee nodded in silence.

They hadn't gone more than fifty feet when a voice coming from behind her stopped Ava in her tracks. "We got a problem," Ellee whispered.

Slowly turning around, Ava saw Ellee pointing to the spot where they had just climbed the gate.

"Straggler," Ellee whispered, pointing to Snoop, who was anxiously watching the girls from the *wrong* side of the fence. Ava let out a sigh of relief, having expected to see something much worse. The dog had accompanied the girls that far, but apparently had not made any attempt to crawl under the fence.

Quietly retracing their steps, Ava whispered to her dog, "Come on, Snoop! Come on, boy!" But Snoop wasn't budging. He just sat there with a confused look that implied, *What am I supposed to do?*

"He can crawl under that fence," Ellee said flatly.

"Evidently, he thinks he can't," said Ava.

"Or he doesn't want to," Brooklyn quickly added, knowing Snoop's reputation for being somewhat rather lazy. Pointing to the gate, Brooklyn said, "I'm pretty sure he can't climb that gate, and I'm really sure we can't lift him over it! Any ideas?"

"We could just leave him," said Ellee, but Ava was not having any of that.

Thinking for a moment, Ava thought she saw a solution. Picking up her butterfly net, she extended the long handle under the bottom strand of the barbed-wire, and using the handle for leverage, pried up the wire. Even though the wire was tightly stretched, Ava was able to pry the bottom strand up a couple of inches.

"Come on, Snoop," Ava implored, "I can't hold this up all day!" But for some reason, the dog just sat there. With her arms getting tired, Ava let the wire relax.

"Let's just leave him," Brooklyn said, somewhat annoyed, now agreeing with Ellee,

"Wait a minute," Ellee said abruptly. "I think I know what might work."

Taking off her backpack, she opened it up and took out a self-sealing plastic bag containing several slices of bread she had swiped off the breakfast table that morning. "I brought these to feed to the little fish," she said. Breaking off a large piece, she added, "But we'll still have plenty left."

Upon seeing the bread materialize out of nowhere, Snoop's ears perked up.

"Pry that fence up again," Ellee instructed.

With Ava now prying the fence up again, Ellee held out the piece of bread toward Snoop. Without hesitation, the dog squeezed under the fence, securing his prize.

Letting the tension off the wire, Ava quietly scolded her dog. "Really, Snoop? You held out just for that? You need to go on a diet!"

"I don't think he knows what the word 'diet' means," said Ellee, smirking.

Kneeling down to examine Snoop's back, Brooklyn said, "Doesn't look like he scraped off any hair."

Ellee, kneeling down as well, carefully patted Snoop down from head to tail, much as a doctor might examine an injured patient. Not finding any apparent damage, she said, "No wonder your dad calls him the 'world's largest beagle'. He's huge!" she whispered. They all laughed. Ava had to once again remind them to hold it down.

Munching on the piece of bread, Snoop seemed unconcerned about the wisecracks concerning his supposed weight problem.

"I think he knew all along you had that bread in your backpack," Ava said to her cousin.

"I think so, too," agreed Ellee.

"Well, at any rate," Ava said, affectionately scratching Snoop's ears, "he might not be fit and trim, but he is sort of smart."

Standing up, getting ready to move once again, Ava made a fist and extended her arm out toward the other two girls. "For luck," she said.

Each girl alternately placed their fists, one on top of the other, making what the girls called a 'stack'. With the stack complete, Ava mouthed the words, "One, two, three," and the girls raised their arms together in mock triumph. Normally, this would be the noisiest part of the ceremony, but this time no one made a sound.

With the expedition now at full strength, they once again picked up their equipment and fell in line with Ava in the lead, but this time, with Snoop now bringing up the rear. Ava quickly checked her cell phone. It was only ten a.m. Needing to be back around three, Ava figured that they had more than enough time to explore this section of the meadow, even if they ran into trouble of some kind.

Still, as they headed out, Ava couldn't shake the uneasy feeling she had in the pit of her stomach. Did she forget anything? What was going to happen? Was the bull going to show up?" It was too late to worry now. She quietly prayed that the 'stack' would indeed bring them good luck.

Chapter 10
X Marks the Spot

The girls stuck close to the creek as Ava had planned, following it further and further up into the meadow, towards the foreboding woods. Eventually, near the creek, they came upon the remains of a giant fallen tree. The huge log made an inviting spot to sit and rest awhile.

The creek, at this point, seemed to slow even more, widening out into the largest pool the girls had seen so far. The pool, however, looked shallow, probably no more than knee-deep. The area around the log and along the bank was blanketed in a mass of wildflowers. The flowers growing behind the log were nearly four feet tall. Most of the blooms were a bright pink color but some were a sunny yellow. All the blooms, however, were splattered with the same small, circular, brown and white spots, making Ellee think these flowers were all the same type, just having different color variations.

"This looks like a good spot," whispered Ava. "Let's sit here and rest a bit," she added.

"Good idea," said Ellee. "It's already getting pretty warm and this backpack seems to be growing heavier by the minute." She slid it off her shoulder and set it down on the grass by her feet.

Examining the tall flowers, Brooklyn asked, "Are these wild daisies?"

"I don't think so," responded Ellee. "They look something like daisies, but I don't know that I've ever seen daisies growing in the wild with these different colors." she added thoughtfully.

They all sat down on the log to take a break. Ava leaned her butterfly net against the log, and Brooklyn followed suit. Ava pulled the radio out of her pocket and said, "I better check in with Izzy."

The three girls looked back to the south. From where they sat, they could still see the second story of the farmhouse, its white paint shining like a beacon of safety in the mid-morning spring sunshine, and the window where they hoped Isabelle was still sitting.

Holding up the radio close to her mouth, Ava once again pressed the transmit button. "Can you see us, Isabelle? Over," she asked. There was a momentary lapse, then Ava's radio came to life.

34

"Still here," she replied with a mouthful of candy. Found any bugs yet?" Isabelle asked.

"No, not yet. We just sat down, but we think this spot looks really good too. We are going to sit awhile and hopefully something will show up, over," Ava said.

"Before you ask," Isabelle replied, "I still don't see nothing that looks dangerous to me."

"That's good. Thanks, Isabelle. You're doing a super job. Keep watching. Over." Ava said.

"Okay Ava. You can count on me," Isabelle replied, as she went back to drawing and munching on candy.

Putting the radio back in her pocket, Ava said to Ellee, "I can't believe she's still sitting by the window watching." The girls all shook their heads in amazement, feeling somewhat secure in the fact that so far, this part of their plan seemed to be working.

After sitting on the log for several minutes, Brooklyn lamented, "This is turning out to be harder than I thought it would be."

"Tell me about it!" whispered Ava. "The few dead insects I've fished out of our lake the past several weeks or the ones that I've found on the ground around the barn, so far have all turned out to be things that have already been turned in by my classmates."

"Ellee then asked, "What are you going to do if we catch something live that you can use? You going to take it to school?"

Ava thought about that for a moment before answering, "I really don't know. I have a chance to get the only 'A' in my class for this last grading period, but my teacher has a policy that if you don't turn something in for the class project, you don't qualify for an 'A'. The best you can earn at that point is an 'A-minus'."

Continuing, Ava said, "Brooklyn and I have caught a few interesting insects lately, but after taking them home and identifying them, I always seem to wind up letting them go."

"The 'CPR' thing?" Ellee asked.

"Yeah, the 'CPR' thing," Ava replied, smiling half-heartedly.

The conversation at this point dropped off somewhat as the girls went back to watching and waiting. By bringing up the topic of CPR, Ellee had inadvertently brought up past memories for Ava; mostly good memories, but one memory Ava wished she could forget, which she now began to reflect upon.

Becoming restless and needing something to do, Ellee produced from her backpack a strip of 'five-mile' orange cloth. Standing up, she tied the strip of brightly colored cloth to a limb above her head on a nearby sapling tree.

"What are you doing?" asked Brooklyn.

"This is such a good spot, I'm just making it easier for us to find it again it we ever decide to come back. We ought to be able to see this from a long way's off!" she said, pointing to the marker.

"That's a good idea," said Brooklyn, giving Ellee 'knuckles' for thinking ahead.

For some reason, though, Ava didn't notice the bright orange marker. Ava had slipped deep into thought.

Chapter 11
The 'CPR' Thing

Sitting on the log, lost in thought, Ava remembered the times she and Brooklyn recently had brought home specimens in her collection jar. Sometimes it would be a pretty butterfly, but usually it was some type of crawling insect that had been easier to catch.

Her collection jar was simply a large, clear plastic jar with a screw-off lid. Her father had washed it out and had punched holes in the removable lid, so the captured occupants in the jar could still breathe while the girl's process of identification was taking place.

Once home, Ava would research the insects on her computer and Brooklyn would scour the numerous picture books they had on butterflies and insects for a match. Sometimes Ellee and Isabelle would be over, and they would help as well. Whether a correct identification was obtained or not, as always, and before bedtime, Ava would creep down the stairs, sneak out the back door onto the deck-porch and release the creatures into the cool night air. Even though the specimens might have been something she could have turned in for her class project, Ava hated seeing her 5th grade science teacher, Mr. Holland, put her classmate's live specimens in his 'kill jar'. Personally, she would not give him the chance to do that to one of her friends again.

Once on the back porch, she would remove the lid and watch as the tiny creatures would crawl up and out of her jar, resting momentarily on the lip, while fanning their wings before flying off to freedom. Somehow, Ava always imagined that this was their way of saying, "Thank you for letting me go." After returning to bed, Ava always felt satisfied and somewhat relieved, after completing this necessary ritual.

Ellee, who had been watching Ava and wondering what she was so deep in thought about, broke the silence. "Ava," Ellee whispered, "what happened to you in Mr. Rocker's class when you were in the third grade? Brooklyn has filled me in on parts of it, but I'd like to hear the whole story from you."

Ava, her train of thought now having been interrupted, swallowed hard, remembering that horrible day.

"Well," she began, "as you just said, it happened two years ago when I was in the third grade." Choosing her words carefully, she continued. "We had just moved into the farmhouse. It was in April, just a few days before my birthday, much as it is right now. My third grade teacher was Mr. Rocker. Everyone really liked Mr. Rocker.

"One Friday, before school was out, he announced that we were going to have 'show and tell' for science class on Monday. He told us that each student should bring in something related to science to show and discuss with the class.

"That weekend, daddy took Brooklyn and me over to the meadow on Sunday. I remember because the weather was beautiful and the meadow was already beginning to recover from the beating the cattle had given it all those years. Daddy had quickly fashioned a butterfly net for me to use, made out of a broom handle, a wire coat hanger, and a pillowcase, but not as good as the ones we have now," she said, pointing to the two butterfly nets leaning up against the log. "However, it worked well enough. He even fashioned a collection jar to put specimens in, the same jar I still have today," she said, now pointing to the jar sitting on the log beside her.

"There were already some wildflowers in bloom and quite a few insects buzzing around that day. We had only been over in the meadow for a short while, when to my surprise, I caught a really large butterfly in perfect condition. Daddy helped me get it safely in the collection jar and we took it home. The butterfly was bright yellow, with black stripes on its wings. Each wing tapered toward the back into what our insect book described as a 'tail'. Our picture book identified it as 'Tiger Swallowtail'.

"Monday morning I took the butterfly in my collection jar to school for 'show and tell'. I gave my presentation right before first recess. Everyone thought my butterfly was really cool, including Mr. Rocker. After my presentation, Mr. Rocker asked me what I planned on doing with it. I told him that at home we always practice 'CPR'. He asked me how in the world that applied to my butterfly. I explained to him and the class that 'CPR' in this case stands for: Catch, Photograph, and Release."

"Oh, now I get it," Ellee said, laughing.

"I then told the class that whenever we catch something at home, no matter what it is, we always take pictures of our catch, then let it go. Mr. Rocker chuckled and said he really liked our idea and had now just learned a new definition for 'CPR'. Mr. Rocker then asked me when I was going to release my butterfly, and I told him I would let it go when I got home. After my presentation was over, Mr. Rocker told me I could leave it on his desk for the rest of the day, so everyone could admire it. After a few more presentations, we all went out for first recess. When we all came back into the classroom, everyone was still buzzing, as was usually the case after each recess. Mr. Rocker came into the room and the class quieted down.

"Someone in the class blurted out, 'Hey, Ava, when did you let your butterfly go?' I looked up and saw that my jar was empty. Mr. Rocker had a bewildered look on his face. He excused himself and went down the hall. In a few minutes he returned with a somber look on his face. He simply said, 'Ava, I need to talk to you after class.' Reading his expression, I knew that my butterfly was gone, but I didn't know at that moment how bad it really was.

"Anyway, after school, Mr. Rocker called me up to his desk, waiting until all my classmates had filed out. He then explained to me what had happened. Apparently, while we were all out at recess, Mr. Holland, the 5th grade science teacher, had walked by our classroom. Spotting my jar sitting on our teacher's desk with the butterfly inside, Mr. Holland thought that my teacher had brought the specimen in for him, for his private collection, as Mr. Rocker was known to do on occasion. Mr. Holland took my butterfly to his room, put my butterfly in his 'kill jar', and then returned my now empty jar back to our classroom, setting it on my teacher's desk.

"My teacher took the blame for the whole thing and tried to comfort me as best he could, but I still cried all the way home. I didn't blame him though. From that moment on, I was pretty sure that I did not like Mr. Holland one bit. When daddy got home after work that night, mommy told him what had happened, and daddy was really mad. He said he ought to make a giant kill jar, big enough to stuff Mr. Holland into, just to see how he would like it.

"The next day at school, several boys in my class leaned over and whispered to me that this Halloween, they would get even with Mr. Holland for me. I appreciated all the support I was getting from my classmates, but it didn't really help. Nothing would bring my butterfly back and I wasn't sure what type of prank the boys were planning. The immediate picture in my mind was one of soaped car windows and rolls of toilet paper hanging from Mr. Holland's trees. This vision made me feel a little better, but strangely, somehow, also a little bit guilty as well. However, I didn't ask the boys any questions."

Sensing that Ava was finished, Ellee then asked, "So what's all this about your 5th grade science project, anyway? Why is this such a big deal?" she asked.

"Well," Ava began again, "if all this isn't bad enough, I learned later that week that when you enter the 5th grade, you might get assigned Mr. Holland for 'Homeroom'."

"Wait," said Brooklyn, "homeroom doesn't sound so bad."

Ava gave the girls a sympathetic look. She explained. "In 5th grade, Homeroom period is where you have science class. So if you have Mr. Holland for Homeroom, you will have Mr. Holland for science as well, and then you will be involved in his pet insect project!"

"And to make matters worse," directing this comment to her sister, Ava said, "Mr. Holland collects small antique farm tools. Ever since he found out that our parents bought Mr. Gray's dairy farm, he keeps asking me if I've seen any old farm tools lying around in our barn! Every time he asks me, I just flatly tell him 'no', but he keeps asking anyway. And there's even more, but I can fill you in on that later," Ava said.

"Even more?" Brooklyn exclaimed, looking truly worried.

Ava paused for a moment, letting the information sink in, as she could see her sister and cousin were already attempting to figure the odds of being assigned Mr. Holland for Homeroom teacher next year.

"So really, no fooling, there's a good chance that we might get Mr. Holland for Homeroom next year?" Brooklyn asked with real worry now on her face.

"You got it!" Ava said. "Unless he gets fired, retires, moves, or dies unexpectedly. In just a few short months, you both might have the same problem that I have right now."

Brooklyn and Ellee just stared at each other in disbelief. That fact that they might get the person who was apparently the most disliked teacher in the school system was almost too much for the two cousins to comprehend.

This fact prompted Brooklyn to ask, "Ava, do you think daddy was kidding about the 'giant kill jar'?"

Chapter 12
Little Miss Awesome

After Ava had finished, the girls refocused their attention on the surrounding flowers.

Ava lamented, "I wish we had something to drink. My throat is really dry!"

"Yeah," agreed Brooklyn, "mine too."

Sliding off the log, Ellee knelt down and unzipped her backpack. She began taking items out, one by one, apparently trying to get at something in the bottom of her pack.

"What are you looking for?" asked Ava.

"Just a minute," replied Ellee, almost to the bottom of her pack. Finding what she was looking for, Ellee produced three bottles of partially frozen water, handing one each to Ava and Brooklyn and taking one for herself.

Open mouthed, Ava simply said, "You're awesome, Ellee!"

Ellee just smiled, apparently having heard that before.

"My bottle's still cold!" exclaimed Brooklyn, holding it up for them to see. "There's still ice in here!" she said, astonished. "Now I know why your pack was so heavy," she added.

"How did you manage that?" asked Ava, referring to the ice.

"Put'em in the freezer at your house last night. Gave one to Izzy, too, before we left," Ellee said.

Ava immediately changed her mind on the necessity of Ellee bringing her heavy backpack along. At any rate, though, it had just gotten considerably lighter.

"Remember," Ellee said, "don't forget to give me back your empties when you're through. Don't want to leave our trash lying around, especially plastics."

Gratefully sipping their cold waters, her cousins simply gave her a thumbs-up.

Momentarily, Ava asked, "Ellee, why do you have all that stuff in there?" She looked at all the items scattered on the ground.

So far the items laid out included: a digital camera, a cell phone, a small first aid kit, one small can of bug spray, one tube of sunscreen, a pack of fresh batteries, one pair of dry socks, one pair of sunglasses, several tubes of lip gloss, and even a pair of women's size 5 flip-flops.

Seeing her cousins' astonished faces, before they could ask the next logical question, Ellee said, "I take all this stuff when Izzy and I go camping with mommy and daddy." Glancing back down into the backpack, she said to their amazement, "There's more."

Ava waved her off. "It's all right, we believe you."

As Ellee began to repack all the items, in a matter-of-fact tone she said, "Daddy always says it's better to... "

Ava cut her off again, laughing.

"I think we've heard that one before," she said, rolling her eyes once again.

"Yeah ," said Brooklyn. "In fact, I think maybe you've taken that statement to a whole new level!" she said, laughing as well.

"But it is hard to argue with what your dad says," Ava added quickly. "Especially now," as she held up the nearly empty bottle of water.

"One question," said Ava. "I get most of the items in there, but what are the flip-flops for? Those look too big for even you to wear."

"Right," said Ellee. "Mommy left these at the beach the last time we went swimming. I picked them up and put them in my pack. I just forgot to take them out and give them back to her."

"Oh, okay," responded Ava. Now realizing the implications of Ellee's last statement, Ava once again asked, "So you even take your backpack to the beach as well?"

"Of course," she replied.

The only thing Ava and Brooklyn could think of to say was, "Ellee, you're too much! You're just awesome!"

With her backpack once again squared away, Ellee asked, "You guys want to feed the fish now?

At the mention of more food, Snoop's ears perked up.

Chapter 13
The Titanic Has Hair

Leaning over, Ellee took out the plastic bag containing the remaining slices of bread from a side pocket in her backpack. Handing a slice to both Ava and Brooklyn, the girls tore them into small pieces and began casting them into the water near the bank.

Almost immediately, small fish came to the surface and began nibbling on the floating crumbs. Upon seeing this apparent waste of perfectly good food, Snoop sidled up to Ellee in order to keep a closer eye on what he probably thought was his rightful share of the bread.

Patting Snoop's head, Ellee whispered, "You're not getting any more, Snoop. You've already had a piece."

Apparently not satisfied with that answer, Snoop decided to take matters into his own 'hands'.

Walking to the edge of the water, he waded in and began licking up the bread crumbs that were still floating on the surface.

"Snoop! You can't possibly be that hungry!" scolded Ava.

"Good thing the water is shallow," said Brooklyn.

"Why is that?" asked Ellee.

"He doesn't swim very well," said Ava. "Daddy says he swims like the Titanic!"

Ava and Brooklyn laughed, having witnessed this before.

However, Ellee was confused. She asked, "The Titanic?"

"Well," Ava explained, "when we put him in Papaw's swimming pool, he swims great for a sum total of about five feet, then he slows almost to a stop. At this point, his rear end starts to sink, and then the rest of him starts to go under, fast!"

"Like the Titanic!" Ellee said, getting the idea.

"Right," said Ava. "If someone's not in the pool with him, he would drown."

"And," Brooklyn added, "there aren't even any icebergs in Papaw's pool!"

Eventually the bread crumbs ran out, either by being eaten in the miniature feeding frenzy between the fish and Snoop, or by becoming too soggy to float any longer. Finally, looking pretty satisfied with his aquatic accomplishment, Snoop emerged from the shallow water.

"I don't think I've ever seen your dog exert so much energy for such a small reward," said Ellee.

"You ought to see what he'll do for a dog biscuit!" exclaimed Brooklyn.

"Yeah, it's pretty sad," Ava said, shaking her head.

"Maybe when we get back, you should enroll him in a class," said Ellee, "where they teach you about what they call 'risk/reward'."

"Risk/reward?" asked Brooklyn.

"Yeah, it has something to do with how much you would be willing to risk on something, compared to how much reward you would receive in return. For example, your dog probably doesn't understand he could drown trying to get those few measly bread crumbs out of the water." He's risking too much for such a small reward. Get it?"

"Yeah, I see what you mean," said Brooklyn.

Scratching Snoop's belly, Brooklyn said, "Hear that, Snoop? When we get back home we're gonna send you to school!"

"Don't sign him up for home economics," Ellee joked. "He'll never turn in a completed assignment."

"That's right!" laughed Ava. "He'll have his assignments eaten before his teacher has a chance to grade them!"

Snoop hadn't heard a word of this latest round of wisecracks once again being directed his way. Since emerging from the water, by rolling around on the soft grass, he had cleaned all the mud off his 'undercarriage' and was now lying on his back, feet sticking up in the air, fast asleep.

"Awww… poor Snoop!" Brooklyn said, kneeling down to scratch Snoop's belly.

"Nothing like a well-deserved nap after a long morning swim," Ava added.

Chapter 14
Trapped

Finishing up their waters, Ava and Brooklyn handed their empty bottles back to Ellee, who promptly stored them away in her backpack. Ava again checked in with Isabelle. Everything still seemed to be all right.

"Good," said Ava. She checked her cell phone: eleven a.m. They had plenty of time to keep looking, and still be back in time to help her mother with preparations for her party. However, looking to the north, Ava was still apprehensive about getting too close to that shed.

She was about to stand and get the other two girls moving again, when a sudden movement caught her eye. Brooklyn and Ellee saw it too.

A rather sleek, strange looking insect had just landed on the tall flowers directly behind the log they were sitting on. Right away, Ava could tell it was something unusual, something she had never seen before, even in their picture books.

Before Ellee could get her camera out, Brooklyn, in one quick motion, swung her butterfly net in the creature's direction. Rather than capturing the insect in the netting, it was knocked off the flowers, landing out in the knee-deep water.

The insect tried to lift off the surface of the water by furiously beating its wings, but its wings had become wet. It continued to struggle. In its attempts to fly off, the insect only accomplished drawing more attention to itself by creating a loud buzzing noise, while at the same time greatly disturbing the surface of the otherwise calm water.

Almost immediately, the girls could see the small fish rising to the surface, encircling the helpless creature.

"Ava!" Brooklyn and Ellee cried out. "The fish are going to eat it!"

In an instant, reaction overcame reason, as Ava leaped into the pond, creating a huge splash. Frantically looking around, she found she was merely inches away from the struggling insect. With the commotion having scared off the fish, Ava reached down with a cupped hand and scooped the creature up and out of the water, not even considering whether or not in might sting her.

Raising her hand, the water cascaded through her fingers and down her arm. Opening her hand, the creature did not seem alarmed. It blinked its large, green eyes at Ava and started fanning its wings in an attempt to dry them off.

The insect, to Ava, didn't appear to be dangerous as it crawled around on her hand, every now and then looking up at Ava, into her green eyes. At that moment, Ava instinctively knew the creature was not going to harm her.

"I think he likes you," Ellee said.

"I think so, too," Ava replied, giggling, as the insect was now starting to crawl up her arm. "That tickles!" she exclaimed. Astonished that the insect did not make any attempt to escape, Ava said, "I think I have a new friend."

The girls watched the insect for a few more minutes. Then, with its wings sufficiently dry, it suddenly rose and hovered in front of Ava for a few brief seconds before flying off to the north, in the direction of the wooded hills.

Ava had that strange feeling again, the one she always had when releasing creatures out of her collection jar at night, that this creature too was in some way grateful for being rescued.

"Wow!" said Brooklyn. "What was that thing?"

"I have no idea," said Ava. "It wasn't the least bit afraid of me. It seemed sort of friendly."

"Am I imagining this," asked Ellee, "or did it seem like that insect was checking you out, just before it flew off?"

"Yeah, that was really strange," Ava said. "Nice, but really strange."

As the girls prepared to move once again, Ellee secured her backpack and Brooklyn picked up the butterfly nets. What they heard next from Ava was certainly not in the plan.

"Hey, guys, I think I'm stuck!" Ava whispered in an alarmed tone.

Trying to move her feet in an attempt to get out of the water, she discovered that she was stuck in the mud.

"Come on, Ava, quit fooling around," said Brooklyn.

"No, honest, look!" exclaimed Ava, as she showed Brooklyn and Ellee how she could wiggle her legs and hips, but her feet would not move. No matter how hard she pulled and strained, her feet would not budge.

At that moment a thought flashed through Ava's mind. She remembered what her father had told them about the creek. "*Whatever you do,*" her father had warned, "*stay out of the creek. It has a clay bottom, and if you get in there, you will get stuck fast and someone will have to come and pull you out.*"

Upon seeing the creature knocked into the water, Ava had just reacted with no thought of the consequences. "Great! Now what?" she murmured.

Realizing that Ava was not joking and really was stuck, Brooklyn picked up one of the butterfly nets and extending the handle out to Ava, said, "Here. Try and grab on to this."

Ava stretched as far as she could without losing her balance, but the handle was too short.

"Try and find a tree limb," Ava said, "or something longer that I can reach."

Brooklyn and Ellee quickly began searching along the bank, but there were few tree limbs on the ground, and the ones they did find were either too short or were rotten. Finally, Ellee found a sizeable limb she thought would work and Brooklyn helped her drag it to the edge of the water.

"This might work, but it's pretty heavy," Ellee said as both girls struggled to get the heavy limb off the ground.

With the limb finally extended out over the water, Ava was able to grab onto the free end.

"Got it!" said Ava. "Hold on tight," she instructed the other two girls, "and I will pull myself out."

Ava pulled slowly at first, so as not to pull Brooklyn and Ellee into the water with her. But with their combined weight, Ava found she could pull much harder. With one last big tug, Ava felt her feet starting to break free, just as the limb broke.

Snap! Ellee and Brooklyn fell backwards, landing on the soft grass. At the same time, Ava rocked backwards, almost losing her balance.

"Now what are we going to do?" Ava asked in frustration.

Remembering that they all had cell phones, Ava could think of only one other option, an option she only wanted to exercise as a last resort. But she realized it was getting to that point pretty quickly.

At that moment, Ava heard Isabelle on the radio. Ava reached into her pocked, pulling the radio out.

"What Isabelle? Ava asked, now dropping the pretense of using the word 'over' when she spoke into the radio.

"Ava!" Isabelle exclaimed, "I saw what happened! Do you want me to go get your mom?"

"Err… hold on a minute, Isabelle," Ava said into the radio. Looking at Brooklyn and Ellee, now back on their feet, Ava asked, "What do you guys think?"

For once, both girls were at a loss for words. Their initial plan hadn't included a water rescue, let alone two water rescues.

Ava, in desperation, took one last look around the meadow, resigned to the fact that she was probably going to have to make the call. Just then she spied the shed, up by the woods, and a thought crossed her mind.

Ava got back on the radio. "Isabelle, we're going to try one more thing. If it doesn't work, I will call you right back."

"Okay, Ava. I still don't see nothing, but I'll keep looking."

"Isabelle," Ava radioed again, with worry in her voice, "if you see that bull anywhere, and I mean anywhere, you call 911 immediately for help! We're gonna need it!"

"Okay, Ava, I will," replied Isabelle. "What's the number?"

Ava just shook her head. "If we need to, I guess we'll have to call 911 ourselves."

Now Ellee spoke up. "What bull? I thought you guys just made that story up so Isabelle would have something to do."

"Well… not exactly," confessed Ava. "We've never seen it since we moved in, but Daddy says it could still be running around loose up here, somewhere around that shed or maybe up there in the woods. Daddy told us that right before we moved in, Uncle Bryan and him helped Mr. Gray round up his cattle. Mr. Gray said that bull had become so mean, they just decided to leave it and wait until they could get more help. Daddy said the bull ran off into the woods somewhere up there," Ava said, pointing to the north. "As far as we know, it could still be in here."

"Great! That's just great!" exclaimed Ellee, now realizing the gravity of the situation.

"I know, I know," lamented Ava. "I'm sorry. I wish I hadn't gotten you guys involved in this mess, but there's little I can do about that right now."

Ava felt the tears start to well up in her eyes, but knowing she was the oldest, she knew she had to fight back the tears and remain calm. She knew it was going to take all of them thinking clearly to get themselves out of this mess. If she broke down now, the others might panic, and she would more than likely be stuck in the creek until her father got home from work, and in that amount of time, no telling what else might happen.

"Now I know why it was so important for Isabelle to know how the radios and binoculars worked," said Ellee. "She really is our lookout!"

"Well, at least she is still taking her job seriously," Brooklyn said.

Ellee was less than amused at that statement, but after getting over her initial anger, she could see Brooklyn's point.

Brooklyn now caught Ava looking to the north, apparently, for some reason, sizing up the area around the shed. Brooklyn did not want to know what her sister was thinking, and she certainly wasn't going to ask.

Ellee had taken out her cell phone and was about to make a call of her own, when Ava said, "Hold on, Ellee."

"Brooklyn," Ava said. Brooklyn looked down, pretending not to hear.

"Brooklyn," Ava pleaded, "I need help!"

Brooklyn looked at Ava, then at Ellee, then at the shed. Somehow, she knew what Ava was thinking and found herself nodding her head, not really wanting to believe it was actually coming to this.

Of the two girls now standing on the bank, Brooklyn was the oldest, being a few months older than her cousin. She knew if Ava was going to get out of the creek without calling their father, it was now up to her to do something. Besides, it was *her* sister that was stuck in the creek.

"Brooklyn," Ava said hopefully, "there might be something up there in that shed we can use to pull me out."

Brooklyn simply turned to Ellee. Taking a deep breath, she said, "You stay here with Ava."

"Be careful," Ellee said, giving her cousin a hug.

As Brooklyn turned in the direction of the shed, she hesitated. Turning back to Ava, she nervously asked, "Ava, there really probably is no bull up there anymore, right?"

"Yeah, that's right. It's probably not up there anymore," Ava said in her most reassuring tone. "You'll be all right, but keep your eyes open just in case. Be careful, Brooklyn. I'll be waiting right here for you when you get back," Ava half-heartedly joked, trying to ease her sister's fears. Both girls gave Brooklyn their best thumbs-up, hoping to build up her confidence.

With that, Brooklyn simply turned and began slowly making her way through the maze of waist-high flowers and grass toward what she knew was certain death.

Ava quickly got on the radio. "Isabelle, come in."

"I'm here, Ava," Isabelle replied.

"Keep a sharp eye out on that shed. Brooklyn's going up there to see if she can find something we can use to pull me out," Ava said.

"All right," replied Isabelle, not believing what Brooklyn was about to do either.

Upon hearing this, Isabelle felt she should say a prayer for her cousin's safety, but she only knew two prayers; the one she learned at preschool that all the kids say before they eat lunch, 'God is great...', and the other one she says with Ellee each night when they go to bed; 'Now I lay me...'.

Isabelle didn't know if either prayer was appropriate in this particular situation, but since those were the only two prayers she knew, she just decided to say both. In her mind, any prayer was better than no prayer at all.

Chapter 15
The Monster in the Meadow

As Brooklyn cautiously made her way through the waist-high grass and flowers, all the horror stories she had heard at school about the 'monster in the meadow' came rushing back to her, making her legs tremble even more.

One incident in particular had happened sometime during the month of October, the year before her parents had purchased the farm. As the story was told around school, it occurred late one Friday night, a couple of weeks before Halloween.

Apparently, four high school boys on the football team had read on the internet about 'cow tipping', and decided it would be a great prank for them to pull this Halloween. Of course, they also thought that their girlfriends, upon learning of their prank, would be greatly impressed.

Now cows are known to be generally docile creatures when left to themselves; slow, somewhat unintelligent, and therefore relatively easy to sneak up on. Evidently, though, in some circles, sneaking up on a cow and achieving this feat somehow becomes a measure of one's manhood.

The process of 'cow tipping' then involves several individuals lining up on one side of the poor, defenseless, unsuspecting animal, who, by the way, is more than likely minding its own business. The pranksters then violently shove the cow over. The cow crashes to the ground on its side, usually to the snickering and laughing of the perpetrators. The pranksters then move on to the next cow, and so on and so on, until they either run out of cows, lose interest in the prank, or get run off by an angry farmer.

The four students in question knew Farmer Gray had a lot of dairy cattle, and since his farm was just a few miles outside of town, they decided that would be the perfect place to pull their prank.

Their thinking went something like this: It was a short drive, almost no one would see them as it would be late at night, and Farmer Gray was in his mid-80s. So even in the unlikely event that they were discovered, getting away from him should present little problem.

They told everyone at school what they were planning, so it was now impossible for them to back out. But they rationalized, "This is really going to be fun. What could possibly go wrong?"

So, as planned, the next Friday night, well after their football game was over, the four drove out to Farmer Gray's property. They parked on the now-deserted gravel road, up by the woods, just to the north of his house. So as not to be easily detected, they didn't take any flashlights, not thinking to simply take a flashlight and just leave it turned off, until you might actually need it.

They carefully groped their way down through the dark woods, eventually coming up to a barbed-wire fence.

On the other side of the fence the students could see that the woods were not as thick and overgrown as the side they were now on, probably due to the cattle that had been eating and tromping down all the vegetation in that area. Looking through this sparse area of woods, to the south, they could see where the woods opened up into a clearing, which they correctly surmised was where the meadow began.

Not readily spotting any livestock to harass, one student noticed an outbuilding situated a little ways into the clearing. "Bet the cows are in there," that student whispered, pointing out the shed. They all nodded.

Not having brought any gloves, which would have come in handy in scaling a barbed-wire fence, they smartly decided not to try it bare-handed. Instead, they decided the best way to get over the fence was to climb up a nearby sapling tree, scoot out on an overhanging limb, and simply drop down on the other side. However, at this point, they didn't give much thought, if any, on how they were going to get back over the fence in the event that they would have to beat a hasty retreat.

Putting this part of their now-improvised plan into action, the first student shinnied up the sapling, climbed out on a limb, and dropped down on the other side with relative ease and minimal noise.

What happened next was not in the improvised plan.

By the time the second student had gone up the tree and dropped to the other side, Farmer Gray's prized 1200 lb. bull, upon hearing his territory being invaded, decided to investigate.

While the third student was still in the tree, they all heard what could only be described as a fire-breathing locomotive charging at them out of the darkness, from the direction of the shed.

Squinting their eyes in that direction, but not yet fully comprehending what was happening, they all instinctively froze in terror. The dark, massive behemoth tore out of the darkness, slamming into the first student who had entered the 'arena'.

The Dragonpillar

Hanging on for dear life, the third student, still up in the tree, watched in horror as the first student was sandwiched between the bull's massive horns, then tossed like a ragdoll into the air and back over the fence, landing on his back with a sickening crunch.

The second student, who, prior to the attack, had also dropped down out of the tree, now realized what was happening and tried to run, but found his legs had turned to Jell-O. The infuriated beast backed him up against the barbed-wire. In an instant, the monster whirled, whipping its hind legs into the air, narrowly missing the student's jaw. However, the blow connected to the student's ribcage, creating an audible 'snap'. This student went to the ground, writhing in pain from having the wind knocked out of him, not to mention the broken ribs he had just sustained.

At this point, the third student, still clinging to the tree, lost his grip and fell into the kill zone. Having witnessed the carnage up to this point, he wisely scaled the barbed-wire fence bare-handed, cutting his hands, legs and arms, while receiving numerous puncture wounds in the process.

Still halfway up the tree, the fourth student, having had the luxury of viewing the battlefield longer than his unfortunate companions, made the group's first (and maybe only) intelligent decision of the evening. Discretion being the better part of valor, he correctly saw the benefit in trying to effect their rescue from the 'safe' side of the fence.

Dropping back down to the ground, out of harm's way, 'Tree Boy' directed 'Slippery Hands', (as he was already cut up), to pull up the bottom strand of barbed-wire.

'Tree Boy' then attempted to reach under the fence and drag 'Broken Ribs' to safety, while 'Rag Doll', who had sufficiently recovered from his launch into orbit, assisted in the rescue.

'Rag doll' began throwing walnuts at the bull, as 'Broken Ribs' was pulled under the fence to safety.

The aerial assault temporarily halted the attack, with the bull backing off, merely amused at what was bouncing off his skull rather than actually being injured by the flying walnuts.

'Broken Ribs' was now out of harm's way, but having just been roughly dragged under the fence, he sustained additional cuts and puncture wounds to the sum total damage already applied by Mr. Bull.

With their fun and excitement now over, the four students, after recovering somewhat, stumbled their way back through the woods, this time without any apparent regard for the 'stealthy' aspect included in their

53

original plan. Cursing and thrashing about, they finally made it to their car, and limped home.

Upon returning home to anxious and angry parents, for their efforts they were all immediately taken to the emergency room at the local hospital. Broken ribs were wrapped, cuts were cleaned and bandaged, bruises were iced, and even several stitches were awarded. Also, as a result of the numerous puncture wounds sustained from their encounters with the rusty barbed-wire, all four students received tetanus shots as parting gifts from the ER nurse.

The next morning, when Farmer Gray went to feed his prized bull, he knew something was up. As he dumped the feed over the fence, the bull strutted out of his stall, proudly displaying his latest trophy; the torn off sleeve of a high school letter jacket, impaled over one of his horns.

Farmer Gray thought it best to go on a body search, but after scouring the surrounding area and finding none, he decided that the trespassers must have survived.

Later that morning though, a family car pulled up to Mr. Gray's house. As the boys limped out of the car with parents watching, from the visible cuts and bandages, it was easy for Mr. Gray to see who the losers were in last night's prank.

"You boys all right?" Farmer Gray asked the combatants, hiding a chuckle.

"Yes, sir," they all answered with bowed heads. "Sorry, Mr. Gray. We learned our lesson. We'll never try that again," they all said in unison, still looking down.

"Yes, I can see," chuckled Farmer Gray.

As no property had been damaged or animals injured, Mr. Gray did not press any charges. Rather, he gave the students a quick lesson in Bovine behavior.

"When you boys get back to school, tell your friends that if they want to do any 'cow tipping', they need to come during the day when the cows are out in the meadow. The cows usually all come back before dark to spend the night in the barn there," he said, pointing to the huge barn just behind his house.

Bowed heads slowly nodded, with three of the boys giving the apparent mastermind of the operation the *you idiot* look.

To add insult to injury, on Sunday, after a longer than normal stint in church, the four students were each presented latex gloves and upholstery cleaner by one upset parent, as they all had to clean the blood and manure from the interior of the getaway car.

By the time school convened on Monday, it was already common knowledge throughout the entire student population that 'cow tipping' at Farmer Gray's was not a good idea.

Chapter 16
Piece of Cake

The walk to the shed was really not that far, but to Brooklyn, it might as well have been a mile away. She moved through the maze of greenery, looking and listening for any signs of danger.

After going a short distance, she broke into a clearing of sorts. Here, something had trampled most everything down. *Not a good sign*, she thought to herself. However, it did make the walking easier and the visibility better.

She wished now that she had asked Ava for the radio. She could have at least talked to Isabelle and gotten an update on what Isabelle was seeing in this area. This would have given her some measure of comfort, as, at the moment, she was totally alone and helpless.

As Brooklyn got closer to the shed, she could see that it was very old, the walls even slightly leaning to one side, as if a giant had been trying to push the shed over, but gave up before the shed totally collapsed. The siding on the shed, being just simple boards nailed over a crude frame, was greatly weathered from being out in the elements over the years without any protection or noticeable maintenance.

Running up the sides, from the ground, weeds and vines had invaded nearly all of the vertical gaps between the boards. The tin roof was completely covered in dead leaves and vines, that over the years, had grown up and over the roof, creating a tangled mass.

Approaching the shed now, the stillness was unnerving. As quiet as possible, Brooklyn crept up to the back side. She attempted to peer through the remaining spaces between the boards, but found the vines and the dark interior too thick for her vision to penetrate. She listened again. The only sounds she could hear were the nesting birds she had just startled as they darted in and out of the tangled vines.

The noise the birds were making made her cringe. "Would the noise alert anything inside to her presence outside?" she asked herself. She waited for the birds to settle down before moving again. Glancing back in the direction from which she had just come, she could see Ava and Ellee. Ellee seemed to still be searching for a longer tree limb and, in a pleading motion, Ava was waving her to go on. Brooklyn turned back, then paused briefly. Before taking another step, she issued a silent prayer for strength and courage. "I need some help here," she said to herself.

She now crept up along one side of the shed, being careful not to step on any dry leaves or twigs. Reaching the front of the shed, she could see that the shed only had three enclosed sides. The front, she was looking at now, was entirely open. She ever so slowly peered around the corner into a mixture of filtered sunlight and relative darkness toward the back.

Glancing now in the direction of the woods, she fully expected to see a woodcutter made of tin, rusted from being caught out in the rain, and unable to lower his axe. But no such apparition appeared.

By now, she was shaking so badly, she was sure that anything inside would surely hear her heart pounding in her chest and her knees knocking together. Every movement she made seemed to be in slow motion.

Nevertheless, letting her eyes adjust to the gloom, she carefully examined the partially illuminated front portions of the shed. She now noticed that the front of the shed did indeed have a sliding door, that a long time ago had been slid open, without ever having been closed again. "Good," she said to herself. "At least she didn't have to open a creaking door!"

Her eyes, now beginning to adjust to the weak light, began to see details of the interior. The side she was on contained an array of small, rusty tools, hung up in rows along the horizontal supports of the shed's framework. The other side of the shed contained a large, fenced-in cattle stall, which could easily accommodate a very large animal. The straw in the stall did not appear to be that old.

"That's not good," she told herself. The straw had been trampled down in a circular pattern, giving it the appearance of a very large nest. The stall itself, on that side, seemed to be constructed along the entire length of the shed. However, toward the rear, a good portion of the shed disappeared into the gloom. Brooklyn did not want to think what might still be lurking or sleeping back there. She fully expected the bull, at any moment, to come charging at her out of the darkness, but there was nothing but continued silence.

Not waiting any longer to find out what might be back there, she crept in, keeping along the wall to her right. Examining the rows of deserted tools, she could see that all were covered in a fine layer of dust. Cobwebs hung from the rafters and spiders stared at her with their red eyes from every nook and cranny, ready to pounce out at her from their silky lairs. This gave the place the unnerving appearance of a real-life haunted house. To make matters worse, as she slowly crept in, the cobwebs clung to her face and matted in her hair. She had to continually wipe them away to see where she was going.

Spiders! Yeeeek! I hate spiders! She cringed, wanting to turn and run, but she didn't. "Why did it have to be spiders?" she groaned.

Staying in the front portion of the shed, lit by filtered sunlight, Brooklyn quickly scanned the walls for something to use. At first, not seeing anything, she began to panic. The gloom, the spiders, and the fear of the unknown were readily taking a toll on her nerves. She took a deep breath, and tried to refocus on why she was there.

Then, in a matter of seconds, but what seemed like an eternity to her, she spied a coil of rope hanging above her head along the top row of tools.

"Rope! Perfect! Now if I can only reach it," she told herself.

Quietly rummaging around in the junk strewn all over the dirt floor, she found an old, metal bucket. Examining it, she found it to still be solid. Placing it on the floor beneath the coil of rope, she turned it upside down, creating an improvised step-stool. Carefully stepping up on the bucket so as not to turn it over, she found, to her dismay, that she was still a few feet short of reaching the rope, no matter how hard she stretched and strained.

Stepping down off the bucket, she again began searching the floor for anything that would increase her reach. Her feet stepped on something. Pulling it out of the dirt, she found she was holding a broken-off handle, about two feet long, from some long forgotten tool.

Quickly stepping back up on the bucket with handle in hand, she extended it up to the coil of rope, placing the end of the handle right beneath the coil where it was hanging on a nail.

"Steady, steady," she told herself as she attempted to raise the coil up and off the nail. At first it didn't budge. She almost lost her balance. She tried again. This time the rope came off the nail, sliding down the handle, ending up draped over her wrist.

At that very moment, the bucket gave way. She lost her balance and fell, kicking the bucket over with a loud *clang!* In what had previously been the stillness of the shed, the noise sounded like a gunshot going off.

Still clinging to the rope, Brooklyn stood up, not bothering to dust herself off or check for injuries. Now, something in the back of the shed started to move. She froze. Her heart leaped into her throat. Peering into the gloom, she couldn't make out what it was, but something was definitely moving around in the dry leaves. It was coming her way.

Not waiting to find out what was emerging from the darkness, she bolted out of the shed and tore around the corner, into the bright sunlight. She beat a hasty retreat, back down the path she had created in the weeds and tall grass on the way up, running as fast as she could while carrying the heavy, musty smelling rope.

Regaining the spot where she had left Ava and Ellee, she tossed the rope down, bailed over the log, and lay flat against the ground.

Seeing Brooklyn running for dear life, Ava and Ellee started screaming, "What is it? What is it?"

Brooklyn, completely drained and out of breath, could only point in the direction of the shed. All she could get out was, "Something's coming!"

Ellee decided it was time to hide behind the log as well. Looking in the direction of the shed, Ava couldn't see anything coming, but she knew something had really spooked her sister. Quickly getting on the radio, she said, "Isabelle, you see anything? Brooklyn just came running back from the shed and she's scared to death!"

"I saw some animals through the binockalars," Isabelle replied.

"Where? What kind of animals?" Ava asked excitedly, now looking intently at the shed.

"I don't know," Isabelle replied. "Small fuzzy animals.They crawled out from under the back of the little house and ran up in that tree."

Ava let out a sigh of relief. A bull certainly couldn't climb a tree, so it must have been a couple of squirrels or raccoons and that's probably what was in the shed that scared Brooklyn.

Ava looked at Brooklyn and Ellee. Having heard the radio conversation as well, they were already getting up off the ground. However, they were still keeping a wary eye on the shed.

As they visibly relaxed, Brooklyn exclaimed, "Whew! That was close!"

Picking up the rope she had tossed down, she said, "This will work, don't you think?"

"Yeah, that's great!" replied Ellee.

Uncoiling the rope, the two girls tied it around one end of the massive log, securing it with several knots. Picking up the free end of the rope, Brooklyn made several loops in her hand, then stretched the remaining rope to the water's edge. Standing on the bank, she tossed the rope to Ava, who easily caught it on the first try. Ava pulled out the slack, then began tugging with all her might. She felt the mud's grip on her feet begin to weaken as she continually applied pressure on the rope. Finally, with one last tug, she broke free.

Hand over hand, she pulled on the rope, until she was able to step out on the bank.

"Ta-da!" she exclaimed in triumph. "I guess daddy was right all along about that creek bottom!" she said. They all laughed in relief.

Patting her sister on the back, Ava said, "Nice job, Brooklyn! That was the bravest thing I've ever seen!" Brooklyn just smiled and for once was speechless.

Ellee agreed. "I wouldn't have gone up there, no way!"

Brooklyn nodded her head in silence, just grateful to be alive.

Brooklyn didn't feel brave. She only felt exhausted. She didn't even know what 'being brave' meant. Right now, she was just too tired to think or care. All she really knew was that she had been scared to death the whole time, but she wasn't about to tell them that.

After composing herself, the only thing she could think of to say to the other two girls was, "Piece of cake."

Chapter 17
The Dragonpillar

Standing once again on dry ground, Ava noticed something just didn't feel quite right. She could feel the wet, sticky muck between her toes and the soft grass on the undersides of her feet.

"Huh?" she exclaimed, looking down.

At the same time, Ellee shouted, pointing down at Ava's feet. "Ava, look!"

"Ava, your shoes!" Brooklyn exclaimed, with a puzzled look on her face.

With mouths agape, the awful realization hit them all at the same time. Looking down at her muddy feet, Ava wailed, "Oh no! My new tennis shoes!"

She had been so preoccupied with just getting out of the water, she had failed to notice that her shoes were no longer on her feet.

"Those were my brand new shoes!" she wailed again, almost in tears, for the second time that morning. They all stared out over the water at the spot where Ava had been stuck.

"I don't think we can fix this one," Brooklyn said gingerly. Now, instead of having one problem to solve, Ava now had two problems to solve.

"Mommy's really going to be mad at me," Ava lamented. "She told me before we left to take them off. I was in such a hurry I just forgot."

Brooklyn said, "I don't think you have to worry so much about mommy. What are you going to tell daddy when he gets home?"

Ava didn't want to think about it. Ava couldn't think about it. The emotional roller coaster of the last few hours was now beginning to take its toll on her.

Ava cleaned off her feet, and the girls decided to rest awhile longer and collect their thoughts. This time, no apparent solution to this new problem presented itself. At one point, Ava caught Ellee looking questioningly at Snoop, and then at the water, then back at Snoop.

"No way! That won't work!" Ava exclaimed, not even letting Ellee get the suggestion out of her mouth.

Looking up, this time Snoop seemed to wholeheartedly agree with Ava's assessment of his limited aquatic skills.

As nothing else came to mind, Ellee decided to change the subject. "Ava," she said, "as soon as you rescued that thing, it flew off in the direction of the woods. I guess it was all right."

"I guess so," said Ava, still pondering her shoe dilemma. Finally, seeing something positive out of the whole situation, Ava said, "Well, I guess it's just as well we didn't keep it. Mr. Holland would surely have hounded me to turn it in for the class project."

They all nodded their heads in agreement.

"I don't think I would have been able to watch it squirm around in his 'kill jar'," she added.

"Yeah, that would have been pretty cruel," agreed Ellee.

Finally, having decided they had done enough damage for one morning, Ava was ready to head back to the farmhouse. They had already pushed their luck to the limit, and still being on the 'shed' side of the fence, they had completely forgotten about Mr. Bull. He could still show up at any moment. Besides, getting back earlier than they had originally anticipated meant they would have more time to help their mother with preparations for Ava's birthday party, and also try and figure out what, if anything, they were going to say about Ava's shoes.

"Oh no!" exclaimed Ava again, now remembering her party that night and all the guests that would be there. "What am I gonna tell Mamaw and Papaw tonight? I know they'll ask."

Ellee, for once, didn't offer any suggestions.

After a few minutes, Brooklyn finally said, "I'd talk to Papaw first. He's always good at fixing things."

"I don't know if even Papaw can fix this," Ava said dejectedly, "but still, it might be worth a try. Thanks, Brooklyn."

As Ava was about to stand, Brooklyn grabbed her arm and said, "Shhh... I hear something."

The girls stopped what they were doing, to listen. No question, it was the sound of buzzing wings, lots of buzzing wings. All of a sudden the tall flowers around them exploded. From out of nowhere, a swarm of the same strange-looking insects descended on the flowers. They began to efficiently

The Dragonpillar

and systematically work their way over each bloom, presumably collecting nectar. Their sheer numbers made the flowers sway to and fro under their weight.

"There must be hundreds of them!" Ellee exclaimed.

Brooklyn reached for the butterfly net again, but this time, Ava laid her hand on Brooklyn's and shook her head 'no'. At that moment, one of the insects landed on Ava's shoulder.

"It's him!" shouted Brooklyn. "Ava, it's the one you saved!"

"Looks like he brought some friends with him," Ellee said, as she reached for her camera.

Straining, Ava was not able to get a good look at the insect on her shoulder, so she held her hand out, palm side up. The creature immediately flew down and rested on her upturned hand.

"It's him, all right," Ava said. "See? He's the only one with those bright pink dots running down along his sides. I remember that. Look. All the rest of them seem to have a different color, but not pink," she observed aloud.

"I think you're right," Ellee said.

Examining the creatures more closely, the girls could see that the insects had large, luminous eyes that seemed to blink at regular intervals. Each had two pair of long, narrow, silvery translucent wings, much like those of a dragonfly. Where the wings attached to their body, they were covered in a shimmering shade of bluish-purple. Behind the wings, toward the rear, their body tapered to a long, narrow tail, colored in alternating vertical stripes of yellow, white, green, and black, much like some caterpillars Ava had seen in some of her picture books. Along both sides of the body, from head to tail, each insect had a row of brilliantly colored raised dots, some all blue, some all green, and some all orange, except for the one insect on Ava's hand. Its two rows of dots were indeed bright pink, and it did appear that this was the only insect thus marked. Each insect also had three pairs of long, slender but sturdy legs. Strangely, each leg ended in three tiny, jointed digits, resembling a small grasping hand.

Noticing this unusual feature, Ava asked Ellee, "You ever see anything like that before?"

"Nope, not that I can recall," replied Ellee, "though some beetles have something like a single claw with a few sharp barbs on the end of each leg, but nothing I know of has anything like this," she said, also pointing to the unusual feature at the end of each insect's leg.

63

"Me neither," added Brooklyn.

As Ellee continued to take pictures, the insects went about their business, paying absolutely no attention whatsoever to the girls.

"But they are insects," Ellee said.

"How do you know that for sure?" asked Brooklyn.

"Because," continued Ellee, "they have six legs, and all true insects have six legs."

"Good observation," said Ava. "You're right."

Now Ava, in order to get more comfortable, shifted her feet, and if that was some sort of signal, the insect on her palm flew down and landed on one of her bare feet. It crawled back and forth over her toes, as if examining them.

"That tickles," giggled Ava. She again held out her hand. Having finished whatever it was doing, the insect flew back up, landing once again on Ava's palm.

"Wow!" exclaimed Brooklyn. "That's really cool! I think he likes you!"

"I think so too," agreed Ava. "I think I have a new friend," she said, smiling at last.

"That's really amazing, Ava," said Ellee, who had been closely watching the insect and its strange behavior. "I've never seen an insect act that way before."

"What do you think they are?" Brooklyn asked.

"Well," Ava offered, studying the insects more closely, "the front part of each insect sort of looks like a dragonfly, especially the wings and the long, narrow legs. But, from their wings on back, they are marked like some caterpillars I've seen in our picture books. Sort of like a Monarch Butterfly caterpillar."

The girls continued to watch the organized chaos taking place on the flowers. Ellee kept taking pictures.

"I got it!" Ava suddenly said. "I know what we can call them. They're Dragonpillars! Get it? Part dragonfly, part caterpillar. Dragonpillars!"

"That's it, Ava!" said Brooklyn, glad to see that Ava was now getting somewhat over the dismay of losing her shoes.

"That does seem to describe them pretty well," said Ellee. "Why didn't I think of that?"

"Ellee, you might be awesome, but even you can't think of everything!" Ava said to her cousin. They all laughed.

At that moment, Ava's radio popped, making all the girls jump. Ava fumbled with the radio, hearing someone talking in muffled tones as she tried to get it out of her pocket. It was Isabelle calling.

"What, Isabelle?" Ava asked, finally getting the radio out of her pocket.

"Ava, the nice man on TV says it's going to rain," replied Isabelle.

Evidently the cartoons were over and the weatherman was on.

The girls looked to the southwest and indeed saw dark clouds gathering on the horizon. "Ok, Isabelle. Thanks. We're heading back now. Over and out." Pocketing the radio, Ava said to the other two, "We need to be heading back."

Just as she finished talking, they heard the rumble of thunder in the distance, coming from the southwest. On cue, the Dragonpillars vanished as quickly as they had come.

"Guess they don't like getting caught in the rain either," Ava said.

Without further delay, they began packing up their stuff. "What about the rope?" Brooklyn asked.

"Leave it," Ava said. "It will only slow us down. We can come back and get it another time."

As Ellee was storing her camera, Brooklyn reached over and pulled one of the empty water bottles out of her backpack. Kneeling down to the edge of the pool, she filled the bottle up half-way with water.

"What are you doing, Brooklyn?" Ava asked.

Without answering, Brooklyn snapped off a handful of the tall flowers and slid the stems down into the neck of the bottle. Her impromptu bouquet was pretty impressive. "For mommy."

"Good call, Brooklyn," Ava said, giving her sister 'knuckles' once again. "Daddy says that flowers always do the trick, and lord knows we are going to need some help when we get home."

As they got ready to leave, Ava looked down at her bare feet. The walk back was going to be painful. Looking up, Ava saw Ellee holding out her mother's pair of pink flip-flops.

"Here, Ava, try these on," she said.

Gratefully, Ava took the flip-flops and put them on. To her surprise, they were a perfect fit.

"Your mom has really small feet!" Ava exclaimed.

Laughing, Ellee said, "I guess so." Ellee was about to say something else, when Brooklyn cut her off.

"Don't say it! No, just don't say it!" Brooklyn exclaimed.

Ava and Brooklyn burst out laughing, then Ellee started laughing as well, finally seeing the humor in it.

"Listen," Ava said in earnest. "No matter what happens when we get back, we at least have to keep the Dragonpillars a secret." She had them both swear never to tell.

At that moment, Ellee, always the optimist, said, "Don't worry, Ava. Somehow, someway, this will all work out."

Giving her cousin a hug, Ava said, "Thanks Ellee, I really appreciate that."

Turning next to her sister, Ava gave her a big hug as well and said, "Thanks, little sister. I don't know what I would have done without you today."

Brooklyn just nodded and smiled, almost tearing up herself.

As the breadcrumbs had run out much earlier that morning, Snoop, who had been taking a nap, and was still asleep, had missed all the excitement. Nudging him with her foot, Ava said, "Come on, Snoop. Time to go."

Waking up, Ava said rather sarcastically to her dog, "You've really been a big help today!" Snoop just ignored the insult.

When the girls got back to the barbed-wire fence, they climbed back over the gate. Without hesitation and without anyone prying up the wire, Snoop belly-crawled under the fence without any assistance whatsoever. The girls just looked at each other in surprise.

"Your dog 'played' us," Ellee said flatly.

"I told you he was smart," Ava said, grinning.

By the time they got back to the farmhouse, it had already started to sprinkle. Before entering the house, taking the flip-flops off, Ava quickly washed the remaining mud off her feet with a garden hose. Isabelle met them at the back door.

"I saw the whole thing!" she exclaimed excitedly. "But what were you taking all those pictures of?" Isabelle then spotted Ava's bare feet and the pink flip-flops in her hand.

"What happened?" she almost shouted.

"Shhh...!" they all implored. Pointing to the stairs, Ava said, "You'll never believe it!"

As Ava, Ellee, and Isabelle headed quickly and quietly up the stairs, Brooklyn ducked into the kitchen. Jill had Ava's birthday cake in the oven and Snoop was already parked in front of the oven door, staring at the masterpiece through the glass panel.

"Don't even think about it, Snoop!" Jill scolded.

Holding out her makeshift bouquet, Brooklyn said, "For you, mommy!"

"Why thank you, Brooky! They're beautiful!" Jill exclaimed. "Where on earth did you find them?"

"Over in the meadow," Brooklyn answered, beaming.

"We'll use them as the centerpiece on the table tonight for Ava's party," Jill said approvingly. Reaching into an upper cabinet, she pulled out a large, crystal vase. Partially filling it with water, she placed the flowers in it.

"There," she said, admiring the finishing touch to the arrangement. Satisfied, she set the flowers on the kitchen table, but not before giving Brooklyn a great big hug.

"I love you so much! Bigger than the sky!" Jill said.

"I love you, too, mommy," Brooklyn replied, not letting go.

With the peace offering delivered, Brooklyn headed up the stairs. By this time, Ava and Ellee had already filled Isabelle in on the small details she had missed. They were now poring over the sketches and drawings Isabelle had made while the others were in the meadow.

"These are really good," Ava said to Isabelle.

Isabelle replied. "I like to draw. I was just passing time."

"You did way more than just pass the time!" Ava exclaimed. "You did an absolutely awesome job with the binoculars and the radio!" Ava patted Isabelle on the back.

"GI Joe helped too," Isabelle said, holding her doll up for the other girls to see.

"Well thanks Joe," Ava said as she shook the dolls' little hand. Isabelle just beamed.

"Hey! I thought I was the 'awesome' one?" Ellee said, laughing.

"She's awesome, too!" Ava said approvingly.

"I like it!" laughed Ellee. "Competition for being the most 'awesome' at our house! This is going to be fun!" she said, laughing again, while giving her younger sister a well-deserved pat on the back as well.

As they went over Isabelle's sketches, Ava was amazed at how much she had done in such a short period of time. There was a sketch of the girls and Snoop leaving; a sketch of Ava climbing the gate; a sketch of Ellee coaxing Snoop under the fence with the piece of bread; a sketch of Brooklyn running down the hill with the rope; and even a sketch of Ava pulling herself out of the water, and several more.

"These are really good, Isabelle. I didn't know you could draw so well," Ava said. Isabelle beamed. "Did you know your little sister could draw so well?" Ava asked Ellee.

"Of course. The refrigerator at home is covered with her drawings. Don't get to look at them very long, though. The art gallery gets changed almost daily," Ellee said, laughing again.

Now, pointing to Isabelles' sketches Ava said, "Now everyone can see what we were up to." They all laughed again, although Ava was worried.

Being the oldest of the group, and the fact that all this had been her idea, Ava knew the responsibility for getting everyone involved in this mess was hers and hers alone. Therefore, she knew the lion's share of the blame would, at some point, fall squarely on her shoulders.

Looking up, Ava saw Brooklyn enter the bedroom. "How'd that go?" Brooklyn shrugged her shoulders. "Okay I guess. Mommy really likes the flowers. You think that will help?"

"I doubt it," Ava said. "Flowers only last so long, then you have to throw them out."

Suddenly alarmed, Isabelle asked, "You think they're gonna throw us out, Ava?"

"I don't think so," Ava replied, reassuring her cousin. "Even if they find out what we did this morning they'll be mad and we'll get punished, but don't worry, they won't throw us out."

The Dragonpillar

The rain began to pound on the roof to the sound of thunder and lightning. Listening to the steady downpour on the roof, the girls became lost in thought, emotionally worn out from the morning's adventure.

Chapter 18
Rock, Paper, Scissors

The girls took time out to listen the rain and thunder. Ava wished the rain would wash away her troubles, but she put little faith in that thought. As the pounding rain let up slightly, Ellee broke the trance the storm had put the girls in.

"Ava, there's still something about your science project that I don't understand," she said.

"Like what?" Ava asked.

"Well," continued Ellee, "it seems to me that with only twenty-four kids in your class, it doesn't seem like it would be that difficult to find an insect that no one else had turned in."

"You're right about that part, Ellee," Ava said, "but here is where I made my mistake. The day Mr. Holland announced the project, I didn't think it was going to be that difficult either. However, when I got to his class on Monday, I realized my mistake. Mr. Holland had written on the blackboard the names of every student that had already turned something in that day and what they had turned in. When I looked at the blackboard, there were so many names listed! At that point, I realized that it wasn't just my class turning in specimens for the project, but all the students in all of his classes! Evidently he didn't mention that on Friday or I just didn't understand what he had said. Either way, most of the students had gone out that weekend, and found something to turn in. Now, most of the common insects had already been turned in and that left myself and a few other students competing for what was left, and as you know, a lot of insects don't appear until later in the spring or summer, so that made it much more difficult."

Ellee thought about that for a moment before asking again, "So every time someone brought something in that they could get credit for, your teacher would write it down on the blackboard beside that student's name?"

"That's right," Ava said. "That way all the students could see what was already turned in, and then you wouldn't waste your time trying to catch something that you wouldn't get credit for."

"That makes sense," Ellee said.

"Anyway," said Ava, "the day the project was announced, it wasn't to be completed for six weeks, so it didn't cross my mind that I needed to get out that weekend and find something. When I got to my homeroom period on Monday, the blackboard was covered with the names of all the students who had already turned in specimens. I was shocked and right away realized my mistake. Apparently, the kids in his other classes knew what to do."

"I see," said Ellee. "That has made it harder to find something."

"Yep," said Ava, "but I'm not going to give up just yet. I want to be the student in my class who gets the 'A'."

"What do you mean, gets the 'A'?" questioned Ellee again.

"Well, you're not going to believe this," said Ava, "but Mr. Holland only gives out one 'A' letter grade in each of his classes."

"You've got to be kidding!" exclaimed Brooklyn.

"Not kidding," said Ava. "Even if, say, four students in the same class period all have grade point averages high enough to earn them an 'A', only the student with the highest grade point average will get the 'A'. The other three would get an 'A-minus'."

"That's ridiculous!" said Brooklyn. "Who grades like that these days?"

"Well," said Ava, "he does."

Thinking about that for a moment, Ellee then asked the next logical question. "What would happen if the top two students in the same class had exactly the same grade point average? What would happen then?"

Mulling over this possible scenario, Ava answered, "Good question. I don't really know." Throwing out some possibilities, Ava said, "Maybe arm-wrestling... flip-of-a-coin... Simon says... take your pick, I really don't know."

Just then, Brooklyn said excitedly, "I know! Rock-Paper-Scissors!"

"Yeah, that would probably be the one," they all agreed, shaking their heads in disbelief.

At that moment, Jill yelled up the stairs, "Girls, time to come down and help!"

Isabelle carefully put away her sketches and Ava put the radios back on the recharging unit. Looking around the bedroom, Ava sighed. The girls then headed down the stairs to help with preparations for what was going to be a very interesting birthday party.

Chapter 19
The Storm

That evening the guests started arriving early, around five-thirty p.m. As it was still raining, plans for the cookout had been moved indoors. Food was being grilled in the garage, then brought inside. Two drop-leaf inserts had been added to the already long dining room table, making ample room for the additional family members that would be attending. Extra chairs had been brought up from the basement and in from the 'deck-porch' and placed around the table as well. A separate table had been set up off to one side for Ava's birthday cake and presents. Brooklyn's bouquet, sitting now in the middle of the dining room table, made a striking centerpiece.

The guest list included: Uncle Bryan and Aunt Lee Ann, Mamaw and Papaw, Peepaw Jeff and Traci, Grandma Barb and George, Ava's aunt Alicia, and Ava's aunt Kristin and her daughter Drew. Drew was Ava's other cousin, who was the same age as Ava and attended the same school.

When dinner was served, Ava, being the guest of honor, was seated at one end of the large table, surrounded by the other four girls. The adults occupied the remaining seats in no particular order. Snoop had already staked out a spot under the dining room table, near Ava, waiting for the usual under-the-table handouts.

During the meal, the girls talked quietly amongst themselves. Occasionally, Isabelle and Drew would break out giggling, but Brett noticed that Ava, Brooklyn, and Ellee were more subdued than one would expect at a birthday party. Brett noticed, exchanging glances with Jill, that she was aware of this as well.

As the meal was served, the adults were engaged in conversation in small groups around the table. It seemed to Ava that when the adults got together, they always talked about the same things.

The men talked about sports, their cars, work, the weather, gas prices and hunting. The women, though, seemed to have a few more topics to discuss. They talked about their kids, school, work, cooking, and shopping. The topic of shopping seemed to be the mother of all topics as it would include, but not be limited to: clothes, shoes, make-up, fashion, home interior, home repair, redecorating, hair color, nail polish, weight loss, weight gain, food prices, best places to shop for bargains, and of course, coupons. Tonight it seemed like the topic of coupons reigned supreme.

Ava hoped the conversations would stay on these topics, but she knew the spotlight would be turned on her soon enough.

As everyone finished their meal, the small talk around the table began to wind down. Several family members began commenting on the beautiful centerpiece.

"Where did you get the beautiful flowers?" several women asked Jill, while looking approvingly at Brett.

Brett simply shrugged his shoulders.

"Brooklyn got them for me today," Jill answered proudly.

"Oh," several responded in surprise, now shifting their appreciative gaze from Brett to Brooklyn.

"The girls went over to the meadow this morning to help Ava find an insect for her class project, and Brooklyn brought those back for me, isn't that right, Brooky?" Jill asked, swelling with pride.

Brooklyn, sensing that any further discussion of that topic might be toxic, just nodded.

"They're beautiful," the guests said to Jill. "What kind of flowers are those anyway?" several asked.

Not having thought about it much, Jill said, "I don't know exactly. I imagine they're some type of wild daisy."

"Interesting," said some of the others, who hadn't been in on the start of the conversation, but were now focusing their attention on the bouquet.

Ava felt herself start to tense up. *Here it comes,* she thought to herself.

Right on cue, Brett asked, "Ava, did you have any luck this morning?"

With the topic now being switched to the meadow, Ava felt her heart begin to race. It was as if a blanket of silence had been thrown over that end of the table. The question produced a lot of fidgeting, blank stares, and bowed heads from three of the girls. Isabelle now even got quiet. Everyone around the table seemed to be waiting for her answer.

Finally Ava said, "Er… not much, Daddy." As an afterthought, she quickly added, "Snoop went along and he must have scared everything off."

Having finally heard an answer, all the adults around the table eased back in their chairs, evidently accepting the answer offered. To Ava's father, Ava, Brooklyn, and Ellee continued to look as though they had something to hide.

Brett looked under the table at the dog. "Is that right, Snoop? Were you a bad boy today?"

Everyone laughed, except the girls. Drew, sitting near Ava, didn't know what had happened that morning, and couldn't figure out why the other three were acting so reserved. Isabelle, on the other hand, seemed to be back to her usual self. Most four-year- olds are still somewhat insulated from the worries of the world.

Having been questioned, Snoop gave his owner his best, 'I'm innocent' look. It almost seemed to say, "Apparently stealing bread crumbs from lazy fish is now classified as a misdemeanor, which must explain the lack of treats that which, by now, should have already been coming my way under the table."

At this point, it was beginning to rain harder, as it could be heard relentlessly pounding on the roof. The thunder was also getting louder and the lightning more intense as well. Several of the guests said they hoped the rain let up by the time the party was over, so they would not have to drive home in the dark with it storming.

From Ava's answer, Brett was still suspicious, but decided for now to let it drop. After all, it was Ava's birthday party and parties are supposed to be fun. Besides, how bad could it be? No one appeared to be injured, nothing around the house, as best he could tell, appeared to be broken, and the barn had not been set on fire.

Mamaw, upon seeing the girls squirming in their chairs, decided to change the topic back to the birthday party. "Ava, did you get a package in the mail today?"

Here we go again! Ava thought to herself. She cringed at hearing the question she had been dreading all day.

Ava looked down, pretending not to hear. Brooklyn and Ellee began squirming even more.

"Ava," Brett said, "Mamaw asked you a question."

Averting eye contact with anyone, Ava's only answer was, "Yes, it came this morning."

"Well, did you like what was in the package?" Mamaw asked.

At this point Ava clammed up. Jill could see that something was wrong, so she spoke up, "Yes, the shoes came this morning. You love them, don't you, Ava?" Jill asked. "She put them on as soon as she got them out of the box and they were a perfect fit," Jill added. "I let her wear them around the house as long as she promised not to wear them outside, until at least after the party tonight."

With this new revelation, Brett was getting an idea of what probably had happened and why the girls were acting the way they were.

"Can we see them?" asked Mamaw.

"Yeah," all the adults said, "we'd like to see them too."

Ava desperately tried to change the subject. She asked, "Daddy, how was work this morning?"

Brett exchanged looks with Jill. Now it was the guests' turn to start fidgeting in their seats, as they suspected something was wrong as well, and a bombshell was about to be dropped on the party.

Brooklyn and Ellee were practically turning blue from holding their breath. *Hope no asks me any questions*, each was thinking to themselves.

Finally, Jill said softly, "Ava, everyone wants to see your new shoes."

With all eyes on her, Ava was trapped. Defeated, she just dropped her head and quietly started sobbing.

Jill quickly got up from her chair and went over to comfort her daughter.

"It's all right, Ava. What's wrong?" she asked. Ava continued to sob quietly. Consoling her daughter by putting her arm around her, Jill repeated, "Really, Ava, it's okay, honey. What's wrong? You can tell us."

Brett noticed Brooklyn and Ellee exchanging looks. Whatever it was, he was now sure that they were involved in it as well, and obviously it had something to do with Ava's new shoes.

Ava stopped crying, but kept her head bowed, remaining silent. The tension at the table could be cut with a knife. None of the other guests knew what to do or say, so most wisely kept quiet. It was left up to Brett and Jill to sort this one out.

Ellee leaned over to Brooklyn and whispered into her ear, "What do you think?"

"I think we have to show them the pictures you took this morning," Brooklyn whispered back. "At least that will explain how Ava lost her shoes. I think we're caught, so at this point, what do we have to lose?" she added.

Isabelle, sitting close enough to hear the conversation between her sister and Brooklyn, was thinking that now might be the opportune time to see if Snoop needed any assistance under the table. But courageously, she decided against the move.

Isabelle held her ground. Having waited this long to be 'on the team', she was not going to cut and run, just when the going got tough, especially if she could be of some help. She got up from her chair, went over and stood by Ava, all the while ready to sock the first person in the nose who tried to lay a hand on her cousin.

Ellee nodded to Brooklyn and got up from the table. Quietly excusing herself, she disappeared upstairs.

Bryan and Lee Ann, who had also been watching the girls' strange reactions, figured that their oldest daughter was also somehow involved in whatever was going on. But Isabelle's reaction floored them.

"She was not even over in the meadow with the others today," Lee Ann whispered to Bryan. "How could she be involved?" Bryan just shook his head, as much in the dark as the rest of the adults sitting around the table.

With the disappearance of Ellee, Brett surmised that some kind of explanation was forthcoming, so he motioned for the guests to relax and see what developed.

In the meantime, Jill decided to change the subject. She placed Ava's birthday cake on the table and lit the eleven candles. Everyone was more than happy to sing 'happy birthday' and, having recovered somewhat, Ava blew out the candles, making a wish.

Brooklyn leaned over and whispered in Ava's ear. "Not hard to figure out what you wished for."

Ava weakly laughed and nodded her head.

Jill then cut the cake and started scooping out the ice cream. Of course, after serving Ava first, Jill gave Papaw the largest piece of cake with the most icing. Some people in attendance might have gotten the wrong impression that Papaw had somewhat of a sweet tooth.

"What?" Papaw said, looking around the table as he tore into the massive piece of cake, nearly hidden by the huge double scoop of ice cream on top.

Ava just let her cake and ice cream sit, as she had most of her food.

Jill continued serving cake and ice cream while Brett was taking birthday pictures. Ava began opening her presents. While all this was going on, Ellee returned to her spot at the table, almost unnoticed, and set her camera on the table.

Upon seeing her camera, Lee Ann thought Ellee was going to take some birthday pictures of her own, but strangely, her camera remained on the table.

Finally, after all the presents were unwrapped, cards opened and read, and thank-yous handed out, Ellee picked up her camera, turned it on, and found the pictures she had taken that morning in the meadow.

Realizing what Ellee intended to do, Ava started to protest. Brooklyn got out of her chair and went over to stand by Ava as well, now flanked by Brooklyn as well as Isabelle. Putting her arm around her sister, she said, "It's okay, Ava. We have to show 'em." Under the table, even Snoop now snuggled closer to Ava, sensing she needed his support, too.

Finally the dam broke. Ava couldn't take the pressure anymore, and just blurted it out. "It's my fault. I lost my new shoes."

Jill just stared at her in disbelief, not knowing what to say. Brett just shook his head, having already figured that part out. Bryan and Lee Ann just waited to see how their two girls were involved before commenting.

The rest of the family members around the table now understood why Ava had been crying earlier, but now, without saying as much, wanted to know how it had all happened. Now all the guests were back up on the edge of their seats once again, listening intently.

"So, where exactly did you lose your shoes?" Brett asked slowly for maximum effect.

"In the creek," Ava said, looking down. "They're somewhere in the creek, at the bottom of one of those large pools."

"I'm sorry, Mamaw," Ava said, looking at her grandmother who had sent her the shoes. "I just forgot to take them off this morning when we went over to the meadow."

Before Brett could say another word, Papaw jumped in to Ava's defense. "Well, I'm sure there must be a good explanation for all this. Why don't we all have some more cake and ice cream, and Ava," Papaw said, "you can start at the beginning and tell us what happened." Everyone agreed, but groaned at the thought of eating more cake and ice cream.

Ava looked at her mother.

"That's a good idea, Ava. Why don't you start at the beginning and tell us everything while you're getting something to eat. You've barely touched anything tonight," Jill said.

Now, realizing just how hungry she was, she tore into her sandwich, followed by a fresh helping of a 'Papaw-sized' piece of cake, complete with ice cream. For the adults, even though most didn't want it, the second round of cake and ice cream was a welcome distraction, except of course, for Papaw, who really wanted more. Ava was even able to sneak a large chunk of cake under the table to Snoop.

As Ava finished eating, Peepaw Jeff asked, "So, what's this all about?"

"Well," Ava began, settling in, "it all started with my class science project. Every year our teacher, in the spring, has the class put together an insect collection. Everyone has to turn in a different specimen to get credit. If you don't turn anything in, the best grade that you can get for that grading period is an 'A-minus'. When the project is finished, our teacher enters it in the county 4H fair under the class name. From what I've heard, our class has won the 'grand champion' award in the youth category ever since our teacher has been doing this. I guess it's a big deal to him."

Continuing, Ava said, "I've been trying really hard to get the 'A' in my class, but so far, I haven't found anything to turn in, at least not until this morning."

"This morning?" Brett and Jill questioned, in surprise.

"Just wait," said Ellee. "You'll understand in a minute."

"Anyway," Ava said, "Brooklyn and I and sometimes Ellee have been going over to the meadow for the past three weeks, sometimes after school, and sometimes on the weekends, but we just haven't found an insect that hasn't already been turned in." Ava looked around, waiting. No one seemed to want to interrupt the story, so she went on.

"So," now, looking at her father, she said, "you remember that section of the meadow you told us to stay out of, you know, the section where the giant bull is still running around loose, and you told us that if we ever went in there, it would trample us flat, remember?"

Incredulous, Jill shot Brett a suspicious look. "What bull?" she mouthed, frowning.

Now, all the adults were looking at Brett. "Well, uh… yeah," was all the answer he offered to Ava's question.

Grandma Barb whispered to her husband George, "He didn't get Jill the flowers, now this. This is getting better by the minute!"

"Shh… " whispered George. "I want to hear what's coming next."

"Well," Ava continued once more, "since I hadn't been able to find anything, while riding around on the Gator earlier in the month, we could see that the area fenced in with the barbed-wire looked much more promising, with all the flowers and the like, so I decided I had to risk it, and go in there and look around."

Ava now told how she had enlisted the help of Brooklyn and her two cousins and how they had secretly planned to get in and out of the area safely, but once in there, things didn't go exactly according to plan.

"I don't get it," said Uncle Bryan, finally speaking up. "How does Isabelle figure into all of this?" he said, thinking there was still no way she could be involved.

"Well," Ava said, smiling at Isabelle. "We knew she couldn't go over to the meadow because Daddy was working this morning, so I came up with the idea of putting her up in the bedroom window that faces the meadow." Looking at her father, she added, "We each had one of your two-way radios and Isabelle had your high powered binoculars. When we got over there, she kept an eye out for us with the binoculars, and if the bull showed up or she saw anything dangerous, she could immediately warn us on the radio."

"*Now* I remember seeing that stuff on her drawing table this morning," Jill said, thinking back.

"And that's why you were playing with my radios last night," Brett added.

Ava nodded, smiling weakly. Bryan and Lee Ann, at this point, didn't know what to think.

"Sounds pretty ingenious to me!" said Papaw, cutting in.

Brett shot his dad the 'look', apparently not pleased with the comment. Papaw just shrugged it off and went back to finishing his second, or was it his third, helping of cake.

Looking at his dad, Bryan said, "Really! How many helpings have you had?"

Now, holding his hands up and looking around the table with a mouthful of cake, Papaw mumbled, "Who's counting?"

The comic relief seemed to break the tension around the table. Ava got it, but the parents didn't. Papaw was purposely drawing the heat off his granddaughter by placing the attention on himself. After the laughter died down, Papaw gave Ava a wink.

"Anyway," Ava went on, "we climbed the gate… "

"Wait," Brett said, "what gate?"

"Ellee found a gate," Ava said.

"Really!" said Lee Ann, actually not surprised at her oldest daughter's resourcefulness.

"Like I said, we climbed the gate and went in. Eventually we found a good spot to sit and wait. Before long, this strange insect landed on the flowers behind us, and Brooklyn tried to trap it in her butterfly net. But instead of catching it, she knocked it into the water. We were afraid the fish were going to eat it, so I jumped in and saved it. That's how I got stuck and that's how I lost my shoes."

Now everyone around the table seemed transfixed by the story they were hearing. Finally, one of the family members asked, "What kind of insect?"

"We don't know exactly," said Ellee. Handing her camera to her uncle Brett, Ellee said, "Here, maybe these will help."

As Ellee showed her Uncle Brett how to scan through the pictures, Ava continued. "After I got stuck, Brooklyn had to go up to that shed all by herself and find something we could use to pull me out. It was the bravest thing I've ever seen," she added.

Several of the family members seemed to be nodding in approval of Brooklyn's efforts, not forgetting that she also was the one who had brought the flowers back for her mother. Ava sensed the tide starting to turn somewhat in her favor, although she knew it didn't really matter what the other family members thought. It was what her parents thought that mattered. Still…

"When I finally got out of the water," Ava continued, "my shoes were gone." Pointing to the camera, now being passed around the table, she added, "After I got out of the water, a whole bunch of those insects showed up, and Ellee took those pictures."

"Well," Peepaw Jeff said, still trying to connect all the dots, "other than going into that part of the meadow and losing your shoes, why did you not want us to see these pictures?" he asked.

"Because, I don't want my science teacher to find out about the Dragonpillars," Ava said.

"Dragonpillars?" several of the adults asked in surprise.

"That's what Ava named them," Brooklyn added quickly.

"Yeah," said Ava, "I made everyone swear not to tell anyone about them. I was afraid if Mr. Holland found out about them, he would make me bring one in. He puts the live specimens brought to school in his 'kill jar', for the project, you know."

"Oh, okay, I see," said Uncle Bryan. "The CPR thing, right?"

"Yeah, the CPR thing," said Ava, knowing that quite a few of the family members in attendance had no idea what that was.

Brett noticed the confusion on some of the adults' faces, so he explained.

"Whenever we catch anything, the girls always practice 'CPR'; Catch, Photograph, and Release, get it? It's just something we do. The girls don't like to see anything unnecessarily put to death," he added.

"Ohhhhh, I see," they all said in unison, now having another piece to add to the puzzle.

"What happened next?" asked Aunt Alicia.

"Well, when the storm started rolling in, the Dragonpillars just vanished," Ava recounted. "I then had to walk back to the house wearing a pair of your pink flip-flops," Ava said to her aunt Lee Ann.

"My flip-flops?" Lee Ann asked surprised.

"Yeah, Ellee had them in her backpack," Ava said.

"I wondered where those went. Thought for sure I'd left those at the beach," Lee Ann said to no one in particular.

"At any rate, we were going to keep our discovery a secret, but after everything that happened, I knew it was going to be difficult, if not impossible," Ava said. "It's really all my fault. I never should have talked them into helping me," she said, weakly smiling at Brooklyn, Ellee, and Isabelle.

"Well, I must say. That was quite a story," said Mamaw. "Ava, you know we can always get another pair of shoes."

"That's not the point here," Brett said to his mother.

The Dragonpillar

"Well, right, I agree," cut in Papaw, "but you have to be somewhat impressed with what they were able to accomplish, other than Ava losing her shoes."

Brett started to object, but Papaw cut him off again. "Seems to me," Papaw continued, "Ava was presented with a difficult problem, devised and executed a clever plan to solve it, and when things didn't go according to plan, the girls improvised and worked as a team to overcome even greater obstacles! I'd say that's pretty impressive for most anyone, let alone for three elementary age school girls and one still in preschool!" he said, smiling at the girls.

The hushed discussions, now going on around the table, sounded to Ava like most of the adults were somewhat agreeing with what her Papaw had just said.

Brett just scratched his head in exasperation.

Isabelle was thinking that, from the speech Papaw had just given, that maybe he had watched a little GI Joe in his day as well or maybe had served in the military.

Ava was now remembering what Brooklyn had said, that you could always count on Papaw to fix things, or as least put things in a better light. Now, if her parents were just buying it.

There was a break in the conversation, as it appeared that Ava was finished recounting what had happened that morning.

Studying the bouquet more closely, Peepaw Jeff's wife, Traci, asked Ava, "You say those insects were attracted to these flowers?" she said, pointing to the bouquet on the dining room table.

"Yes, why?" asked Ava.

"Well," Traci said, "I worked in a large commercial flower shop for twenty-five years, and I've never seen anything like them. They look like they're a type of daisy, but they're somehow different. Interesting."

Jill, having finished scanning through Ellee's pictures, looked up and said, "I agree. Those flowers are odd, but check out these insects! I've never seen anything like these anywhere either!"

The adults around the table now began asking for the camera back, wanting to take another look at the insects. Ava was hoping that this new mystery might somehow overshadow the topic of her lost shoes.

Ellee now spoke up. "When we got back to the house, we downloaded all of these pictures to Ava's computer. Then we ran the pictures of the insects against a database we found online, of all known insects in North America, and didn't get a single match."

Jill said, "If it's all right, I think I will download these pictures to my computer, then tomorrow I will forward them to Mr. Gordon, the biology teacher at the high school. If anyone knows what these are, it will be him. If not, he knows who to contact to find out. Is that okay with you, Ava?"

Ava started to protest, but her father came to her defense. "Ava, don't you worry about Mr. Holland. I don't care if you get an 'F' in his class. He can't make you bring anything in you don't want to. If necessary, I will personally deal with Mr. Holland. All right?"

"Okay, daddy," Ava said, finally smiling again.

Upon hearing this, Ava remembered what the boys in her class had said about getting even with Mr. Holland. She once again envisioned toilet paper hanging from trees and car windows being soaped, but she was pretty sure her father had grown out of that phase some time ago.

Drew's mother, Kristin, having sat the entire time without saying a word, finally asked, "Drew, did you know any of this was going on?"

"No," replied Drew. "I had no idea at all. I don't have Mr. Holland for any of my subjects. All I ever heard at school was about the bull that lived in the meadow."

With that, the party started to wind down. As people were leaving, Ava made sure she again thanked everyone for coming and for the presents. Ava made a blanket apology to all the guests for ruining the party.

"Don't you worry about it for one minute," Aunt Alicia said, giving Ava a hug. "You didn't ruin anything. I'm sure everyone will agree that your party was the most interesting birthday party they have ever attended. I know it was for me," she said, giving Ava another hug.

"She's right," several guests agreed as they stepped out on the front 'deck-porch', finding that the storm had passed. Lightning could still be seen off in the distance to the northeast, but the sky had cleared and the stars were out.

Standing out on the porch, Ava took a deep breath. Somehow, the air always seemed so fresh and clean after a good spring thunderstorm. The driveway was a maze of mud puddles left by the downpour, and everyone had to splash their way to their cars, honking and waving goodbye, as they drove off.

Ava felt her strength, as well as her sanity, coming back. What Ellee had said might just turn out to be right. So far, it did seem that things might work out after all, even though she knew there would be punishment of some type forthcoming. But at least for now, Ava felt she was up to the challenge, whatever that punishment would turn out to be.

Looking up into the clear night sky, Ava wondered if rainbows ever came out after dark. Squinting at the shimmering stars, she thought she saw the faint outline of one over their house.

Isabelle, heading back into the house, stopped and asked, "What are you looking at, Ava?"

"I thought I saw a rainbow," she replied slowly, pointing at the sky above their rooftop.

Now looking up as well, Isabelle said, "I don't see one."

Both girls stood for a moment longer, searching the night sky in vain. "Oh well," Ava sighed, as she gave up and turned to go back into the house. Isabelle, however, had not yet given up.

"Ava, where *do* rainbows go after dark?" she asked.

Isabelle turned, but Ava had already gone inside, the screen door slamming shut behind her, leaving Isabelle alone to ponder her own question.

Coming back into the house, the girls heard Jill running Snoop out of the kitchen. While everyone was outside saying their goodbyes, Snoop had turned over the kitchen trash can, pulling out all the paper plates that had been used for food, cake, and ice cream at the party. Each plate was now polished to its original factory finish.

That night, after everyone had gone to bed, Jill cornered Brett. "What's this you told the girls about that bull still living up there in the meadow?"

"Well," Brett answered, "I told them that for a good reason. Dad told me when he was around ten years old, his brother got cut up pretty badly while trying to climb a barbed-wire fence at a family Fourth of July party. I didn't want the girls trying to climb that barbed-wire fence we still have up around the north section of the meadow, so I made up the story about the bull still being there so they would really be scared of going in there."

"So," Jill said, "do you think that was a good idea tell them that?"

"Well," Brett said, "it does make you wonder after all that happened this morning. At least they didn't try to climb over the barbed-wire," he said laughing.

Brett continued to laugh.

"What?" Jill asked.

"I was there when they loaded that bull into Mr. Gray's truck. It took eight full grown men and a lot of luck to get it in the back. Several of the men got stomped on and a few got kicked in various places. One guy got head-butted and pinned against the cab! The bull's horns even broke out his back window! Mr. Gray later told me that by the time they delivered that bull to another farm, it had completely trashed the back of his truck. Mr. Gray added that it was truly a miracle that those high school students a couple of years earlier didn't get killed!"

The next evening, being Sunday night, Ava and Brooklyn were again getting ready for bed. Ava got called downstairs. With a somber face, she padded down the stairs, finding her parents entrenched in the kitchen.

"Have a seat," her father said. Ava knew she was about to learn her punishment and apparently her father was going to do the talking. *Not good*, she thought to herself.

After a thirty minute discussion, she headed back up the stairs. As Ava entered the bedroom, Brooklyn, who had been anxiously waiting, asked, "What's the verdict?"

Seeing that Ava was not crying, Brooklyn hoped it was not as bad as they had been expecting.

"Well," Ava began, "they said that first of all, since the idea was mine, and since I am the oldest and should have known better, I am going to receive more punishment than the rest of you."

"We figured that already," said Brooklyn, trying her best to sound positive.

"So, I'm grounded for a week, for starters," Ava said, "through next Sunday," she added.

"What does that mean?" asked Brooklyn.

"When I get home from school," Ava said, "the only place I can go is to softball practice, my softball games, and church next Sunday. Also no video games, movies, or cell phone for a week!"

"No cell phone? That's hitting you where it hurts the most!" said Brooklyn.

"Yep," replied Ava, looking somewhat dejected. "But it's worse than you think. Since I'm grounded, that means I can't go over to the meadow for a whole week, and the deadline for turning something in at school is May 2nd, two weeks from tomorrow! I checked my softball schedule for the last week of April, when I will no longer be grounded. That week I have a game on two evenings and practice two of the other nights. Then my team is playing in our first out-of-town tournament that Saturday. That means at best, I will only have a couple of days left to go over to the meadow to look for something for my class project!"

Brooklyn, who had been taking all this in, said, "I'm not grounded. I can still go and look for you."

"No, Brooklyn, thanks anyway. I don't want you to do that," Ava said. "I've gotten everyone in enough trouble as it is. But, thanks for the offer anyway," she said, giving her sister a big hug.

"What are the rest of us going to get?" Brooklyn asked her sister.

Sighing, Ava went on. "Daddy said that any other punishment handed out will apply, or *be applied*, as he put it, equally to all of us."

"Ouch!" exclaimed Brooklyn. "I don't like the sound of the 'be applied' part!"

Ava added, "They haven't decided anything yet. Daddy said they haven't had time yet to talk about it with Uncle Bryan and Aunt Lee Ann. However, they said it probably wouldn't be much longer."

Mulling this over, Brooklyn said, "This must be what it feels like sitting in prison, waiting for your execution!"

"Yeah," Ava said, "you're right. And I don't think the Governor's going to call with a pardon for us anytime soon."

Chapter 20
Sweet Dreams

Monday morning, as soon as Jill got to her classroom, she emailed Ellee's pictures to Mr. Gordon, the high school biology teacher.

After school, right before Jill left for the day, Mr. Gordon stopped by Jill's classroom. Ava, Brooklyn, and Ellee were already sitting in Jill's empty classroom, chatting and waiting for Jill so put some things away and clean off her desk before going home.

Stepping out in the hall, Jill and Mr. Gordon could be seen having a hushed discussion, apparently about the pictures, the girls thought. In a few minutes Jill came back into her classroom, evidently satisfied by the look on her face that the discussion had ended on a positive note.

On the way home, Jill did not bring up the topic, nor discuss what she and Mr. Gordon had talked about.

That night, having finished their homework, Ava and Booklyn were in their bedroom discussing the day's events. They could hear their parents downstairs in a muffled conversation, apparently in the kitchen from the sound of dishes being put away and the clinking of coffee mugs being refilled.

Soon after that, the girls heard two pairs of footsteps coming up the stairs. They quickly jumped into bed, pretending to be asleep. The door to the bedroom opened, and their parents quietly walked in, knowing that the nightly ritual of the girls acting like they were asleep would soon be short-lived.

Brett cleared his throat, this being the 'signal' for the girls to 'wake up'. However, instead of tucking them in and kissing them goodnight, both parents pulled up a chair and sat down, facing the girls.

"Okay, listen up," Brett said.

"Oh no!" Ava thought. "The rest of their punishment was about to be announced."

The Dragonpillar

Brooklyn, thinking the same thing, still pretended to be asleep, thinking she could somehow escape her sentencing.

Brett reached up to the top bunk, tickling her through the covers. "Nice try, Brooklyn." Brooklyn, being very ticklish, had to immediately give up the act in order to fend off the 'attack'.

"Get down here," her mother said in a surprisingly pleasant tone.

Throwing off her covers, Brooklyn climbed down the ladder and sat down next to Ava and Snoop on the edge of Ava's bed.

This time Jill said, "All right, listen up."

Mommy was going to do the talking, Ava thought to herself. Hopefully, punishment might *not* be the topic of tonight's discussion.

Continuing, Jill said, "I sent Ellee's pictures to Mr. Gordon first thing this morning. As you know, right before we left school today, he paid a visit to my classroom. At first he told me he thought it was some kind of prank, but when he realized that I was the one who had sent him the pictures, he decided he better talk to me and find out more about it. After talking to me out in the hall, I convinced him it was no prank. The pictures on the camera were real, and were taken only two days ago by my niece."

"A prank?" asked Brooklyn.

"He thought the pictures had been faked," Jill explained.

"Oh," replied Brooklyn.

"Anyway," Jill continued, "he said he studied all the pictures, but was not able to positively identify either the insects or the flowers. That's why at first he thought it might be some sort of prank."

The girls sat quietly, taking it all in.

"He called tonight to let me know that he has forwarded the pictures to some friends of his in the science and agriculture department at Purdue University," Jill said.

"Why would he do that?" Ava asked.

"Well," Jill said, "Purdue University has an entire department and staff devoted to science and agriculture, which would include insects and flowers. They are world-renowned in their research and Mr. Gordon said if anyone can find out what these pictures show, it would be them."

"That's pretty neat," said Ava, her interest now piqued.

Ava asked, "What's gonna happen if they can't identify them?"

"Well, Mr. Gordon says they have the world's largest database of known insects and flowers. He said it shouldn't take them very long to get a match once they load your pictures into their computer system. If they don't get a match, that's when it will get really interesting," Jill said.

"Interesting?" Brooklyn asked. "How so?"

"Well," Jill said, "if they don't get any matches, Mr. Gordon said they will probably want to send a team of researchers down here to check this out for themselves."

Brett and Jill could see that this news had gotten the girls really excited.

"So what do we do now?" Ava asked.

"Nothing for now. Mr. Gordon said as soon as the experts at Purdue are finished with their analysis of the pictures, they will call him with their results, and then he will call us."

"Oh, by the way," Brett added, "Mr. Gordon said if the researchers do indeed send a team down here, they will want you girls to go along to show them where you found these Dragonpillars, as you call them."

"Wow! They want us to go?" exclaimed Ava. "That's awesome!"

But just as the words of excitement escaped her lips, she remembered something and her face visibly clouded over.

"But what if they come while I'm still grounded?" she asked gloomily.

"If by chance that happens," her father said, "we'll talk about it. Until then, don't lose any sleep over it."

"Now let's get back into bed and go to sleep," Jill said.

The girls climbed back into bed and their parents kissed them goodnight before heading back down the stairs.

It was difficult for both girls to get to sleep due the exciting news they had just heard, plus the possibility of what might be coming next, but they finally drifted off to sleep.

Ava dreamt of leading a safari through the wild bush country of deepest, darkest Africa.

Brooklyn dreamt she was being chased by angry bulls through the streets of Pamplona, Spain, as one of the brave participants in an event held there every year called, 'The Running of the Bulls'.

Chapter 21
Pink Bobbys

On Wednesday evening, two days after Jill had sent Ellee's pictures to Mr. Gordon, Ava and Brooklyn were again sitting in their bedroom doing homework when then they heard the land-based phone 'go off'.

Ava looked at Brooklyn and said, "Can you believe we still have one of those things in our house, and it actually works!"

"I know," said Brooklyn. "I jump every time it rings. It's so loud!"

Whenever my friends come over they always ask me what that thing is. Then they ask me if it works, and I have to tell them it does," Ava said shaking her head. "How embarrassing!"

"Really!" mocked Brooklyn. "I can't believe that thing still works! It's ancient!" she said, shaking her head as well.

Both girls went back to finishing their homework. Eventually, they heard their mother hang the receiver up on the land-based phone, apparently ending the conversation. A few minutes later, their parents came up the steps and walked into the girls' bedroom.

Looking up from her desk, Ava whispered to Brooklyn, "Wonder what's up now?" Brooklyn didn't have time to reply.

"I just got off the phone with Mr. Gordon," Jill said, addressing both girls. "He told me that he had just gotten off the phone with a Mr. Martin, one of the lead researchers at Purdue University in the agriculture department, who had been in charge of examining Ellee's pictures.

"Apparently," Jill continued, "they did not find a single match for the insects or those flowers. They are really interested in finding out more about what you girls found."

"Wow! That's pretty cool!" exclaimed Brooklyn.

"I knew it!" shouted Ava, gazing out the window. "I knew they were something special!"

"Well," Jill said, "if the weather cooperates, they wanted to know if they could bring a team of researchers from the university down here this Saturday afternoon to check out things for themselves. We told them we didn't have a problem with that, but we hadn't had time to take down any of the fence yet and they would have to climb the gate, as you girls did."

"Awesome!" said Ava. "That shouldn't be any problem."

"And of course," said Brett, "they want all four of you girls, if possible, to go along and show them exactly where you found everything."

Ava looked down, remembering that she would still be grounded Saturday.

Seeing her expression, Brett said, "Sometimes, special circumstances call for special consideration. Your mother and I talked this over before we came up here, and we think it is only fitting that you go along as well," he said to Ava.

"Yes!" Brooklyn said, pumping her fist.

"Well," Brett continued, "before you get too excited, just remember you both still have some punishment coming, and Ava, you will still be grounded for the remainder of Saturday and Sunday," he said. "But in this case, we thought it would be appropriate for you to receive a short reprieve of your sentence."

"So what do we do now?" asked Ava.

"Mr. Gordon said it would be a good idea not to disturb the area or pick any more flowers. He said that if these insects and/or the flowers turn out to be a totally new, as yet undiscovered species, they will more than likely be immediately put on the 'endangered species list' and then be protected by federal law."

"What does that mean?" asked Ava.

"Well, that means that no one will be able to bother them in any way, unless they want to pay a 10,000 dollar fine!" Brett said.

"So when my teacher finds out about them, he won't be able to make be bring one in for the class project?" Ava asked expectantly.

"Nope, not even if you find a dead one," Brett added firmly.

"Yes!" Ava exclaimed. Now she was the one pumping her fist.

"Well," Ava said reflecting, "I still need to find something for my project."

"You know, Ava," Jill said, "it is what it is. You've worked really hard to this point, and besides, you still have a little time to find something before your deadline."

The Dragonpillar

"Yes," Brett added. "We're not proud of the fact that you girls disobeyed, but we are really proud of the way that you, Ava, have handled your punishment so far, and the fact that you've worked so hard to find something for your project."

"You know," he added, "you don't always make every catch, hit every pitch, win every game, or always make straight 'As' every grading period, but the important thing to remember is you never give up and never stop trying to improve, no matter how old you are. But I think you girls already know that."

Both girls thought about that for a moment, then Ava said, "Yeah, Papaw always says 'there is no substitute for hard work'."

"Papaw's right about that," Brett said.

Brett and Jill gave the girls a hug, and headed out of the bedroom.

Turning back, Jill said, "Oh, I almost forgot. Mr. Gordon said that if the insects or the flowers turn out to be new species, then all four of you girls will get credited with the discovery. That means you will then have the privilege of naming your discovery," she said, smiling.

"It seems to me that you've already decided on a name for the insects," she said, "so you might want to give some thought on what you would want to name those flowers, just in case they turn out to be a new species as well."

As their parents headed down the stairs, Brooklyn excitedly whispered to Ava. "I know, I know!" she said.

"You know what?" asked Ava.

"I know what the flowers should be called," she said.

"What?" asked Ava.

"Pink Bobbys!" she said, almost exploding. "Get it?"

Understanding what she was talking about, Ava said laughing, "That's perfect, Brooklyn!"

However," Ava said thinking, "we should run this by Ellee and Isabelle next chance we get. We want them to be a part of this as well, but I like it. Pink Bobbys! It makes perfect sense!"

That night both girls again had trouble falling asleep from all the exciting news they had just received. However Snoop, hogging space on Ava's bed as usual, had no such trouble. He was dreaming of all the 'new species' of scraps and treats he might yet discover in the kitchen trash can.

Later that evening, Brett called his brother, Bryan, and told him about the researchers from Purdue University possibly coming down to the farm this Saturday, if the weather was nice.

"They want all the girls to be here, if possible," Brett informed him.

"Mmm... I don't know, maybe," Bryan said, "if they don't brag about their football and basketball teams beating IU this year. I'm kind of an IU fan, you know," he said.

"Wow!" Brett exclaimed in mock surprise, "I almost forgot! Well, I guess we'll see all you IU fans here on Saturday then," he concluded.

Chapter 22
On Safari

The weather outlook for the weekend was for clear skies and temperatures in the mid to upper 70's, with an unusual dry spell forecast for the coming ten day period. Mr. Gordon called the house Friday evening and said that Mr. Martin and his research team, along with himself, would indeed be down around one p.m. the next afternoon.

Ava and Brooklyn awoke early on Saturday and got their morning chores done in preparation for the arrival of Mr. Martin and his team. Ava ran the sweeper upstairs and on the carpeted steps, while Brooklyn was in charge of vacuuming the downstairs. The girls made their beds, then took all their dirty clothes down to the laundry room. Finally, Ava fed the dog and had to fold all the clean towels in the laundry room. Brooklyn finished up by taking out all the trash and sweeping out the kitchen with a corn broom.

At one p.m. sharp, a large, black, shiny four door passenger vehicle pulled up in front of their house. A second vehicle, a dark green SUV, pulled up as well. The SUV had large, official looking emblems on the sides of both front doors. Red lights could be seen hidden in the front grill.

Bryan and Lee Ann had brought Ellee and Isabelle over earlier and as the vehicles came to a stop, both families came out of the house to greet the visitors. Of course, Bryan was wearing an IU shirt.

As the men emptied out of the black vehicle, the driver walked up and introduced himself as Mr. Martin, head of the research team organized to investigate the girl's discovery. As the other men walked up, they introduced themselves to the families as well. One of the men was Mr. Gordon, the high school biology teacher, whom the parents already knew. The other men, Mr. Martin said, were his assistants.

All the men appeared to the girls as if they were going on safari. All were wearing khaki shorts and khaki short-sleeved shirts, knee-high socks, and all were wearing the same kind of rugged-looking hiking shoes. They even wore matching hats with some kind of emblem on the front.

One man however, was dressed in plain clothes, and was carrying a notepad and a camera with an attached lens that looked very expensive. He introduced himself as Mr. Koonz, a reporter from the local paper. Brett and Bryan knew Mr. Koonz, as years ago he had covered sports teams they had been on while in high school.

The lone occupant of the dark green SUV got out and introduced himself as Mr. Barry, the conservation officer covering the county their farm was located in. He wore a dark green short-sleeved shirt with official looking patches on both shoulders as well, similar to the emblems on the sides of his vehicle. He had on dark green trousers and wore black combat style boots. He also wore a wide, black belt around his waist, to which was fastened a holster containing a firearm, secured in place by a sturdy leather strap snapped over the weapon's handle. Isabelle immediately took a liking to him, thinking Mr. Barry was in the military.

Ava, by now, having thought everyone had been introduced, heard the back door of the black vehicle open again, then close. To her dismay, out stepped her homeroom teacher, Mr. Holland.

"Geez!" Ava muttered. "Why did they have to bring him?"

Ava glanced over at Brooklyn and Ellee. They were giving Ava the thumbs-down sign, having seen him get out of the vehicle as well.

Seeing Mr. Holland appear, Brett and Jill casually maneuvered themselves behind the girls in hopes of keeping the wisecracks down before the girls got too carried away.

Bending down, Jill whispered to the girls, "Just be polite. Mr. Martin must have had a good reason for inviting him."

"That still doesn't mean I have to like it," Ava whispered back.

Walking up, apparently feeling 'late for the party', Mr. Holland did not take the opportunity to introduce himself.

Mr. Barry was the first visitor to actually greet the girls. So as not to intimidate them, he knelt down to their level where he could speak to each girl eye to eye.

The girls immediately took a liking to Mr. Barry. He was polite and was about the same age as Ellee and Isabelle's father. The girls could sense that Mr. Barry was genuinely interested in what they had to say. Shaking each girl's hand, by the time he got down the line to Isabelle, she was standing at full attention, saluting.

"Honey, I'm not in the military," Mr. Barry said, hiding a chuckle.

Thrown off, Isabelle asked, "Are you a cop?"

"Isabelle, that's not very polite!" Lee Ann scolded.

Mr. Barry laughed, taking it in stride. "That's quite all right," he said. "I get that question a lot from children."

Bending down again, he said to Isabelle, "No, I'm a conservation officer."

Afraid to ask any more questions, Isabelle just nodded, pretending to know what that was, when she really didn't.

After Mr. Barry was through talking to the girls, it was Mr. Martin's turn to introduce himself and his team to the girls. Taking a cue from Mr. Barry, he knelt down to talk to them as well. "So these are the girls who took the pictures," he said. "I'm very pleased to meet all of you."

Ava spoke up first. "Well, actually, sir, my cousin here," Ava said, pointing to Ellee, "is the one who took all the pictures, although, all of us were there when the insects showed up, except for Isabelle."

"I see," said Mr. Martin.

Continuing, Ava said, "We were looking for an insect for my class project. When those insects showed up, we thought they might be something special, so I had Ellee get her camera out and take pictures of them."

"Yes, I've heard about your class project," Mr. Martin said, glancing back at Mr. Holland.

"My cousin Isabelle here helped too," said Ava, patting Isabelle on the shoulder, "although she was not over in the meadow that morning."

"Oh," Mr. Martin said. "So if she wasn't there, how did she help?" he asked.

"Well," Ava said, "because she's only four –"

"*Almost five*," Isabelle cut in.

Ava smiled at Isabelle. "She's not allowed to go with us unless an adult goes along, and since that morning none of our parents could go, we had to leave her at the house."

"Okay?" Mr. Martin said, looking somewhat puzzled.

"We set her up by a window that faces the meadow in our upstairs bedroom," Brooklyn said. "She had a pair of Daddy's binoculars and one of his two-way radios. We took the other radio with us."

"Yeah," Ava said, "she was our lookout, so to speak."

"Lookout?" several of the other men asked together.

"Yeah, she was our lookout," Brooklyn said excitedly. "With the binoculars she was looking out for the bull Daddy told us still lives up there in that part of the meadow. Daddy said if we ever went in there, that bull would stomp us flat! And with the binoculars, if Isabelle saw it, she could warn us with the radio!"

"Oh, all right, I see," said Mr. Martin, looking dubiously now at Ava and Brooklyn's father.

"Uh… it's a long story," Brett offered up, shrugging his shoulders.

"Well, at any rate," Mr. Martin said, "you girls certainly seem to be very resourceful."

The girls just smiled.

With everyone now ready to go, Brett pulled the Gator out of the barn, with the flatbed utility trailer already attached. The girls climbed on and they were just about ready to pull away when Ava yelled at her father, "Snoop's not on!"

Brett put the engine in park, got off, and went back to where Snoop was sitting. He had to physically pick Snoop up and put him on the cart with the girls.

"Really, Snoop?" Brett exclaimed. "I bet if the girls had any food with them, you'd find a way to get up there by yourself!" Snoop just ignored the comment and took up his usual spot on the trailer, front and center.

"Ellee leaned over and whispered in Snoop's ear, "Well played, Snoop." The other girls just nodded their heads and giggled.

"Your dog really is smart," Ellee said to Ava. "I wasn't sure before, but I'm convinced," she added laughing.

"Told ya," Ava said, smiling, while giving her dog an additional pat on the top of his head.

By the time the Gator pulled away, all the girls were taking turns scratching Snoop's ears and playing with his tail, as the rest of the adults walked alongside or behind the trailer.

Mr. Holland, who up to this point had not been overly talkative, asked, "Is that dog going with us? He'll probably scare everything off."

Ava turned and glared at him. The other girls followed suit.

Brett, sitting in the driver's seat, stopped the Gator, turned, and said flatly, "If he doesn't go, nobody goes."

The Dragonpillar

Mr. Holland started to say something else, but decided against it. To his credit, he quickly surmised that it would probably not be a good idea to push Ava's father any further, especially when it came to the disposition of the family dog.

Instead, Mr. Holland reluctantly fell in line with the rest of the adults, keeping any further comments to himself as he walked behind the vehicle. After hearing her father put Mr. Holland in his place, Brooklyn and Ellee gave Ava 'knuckles'.

Leading the way, Brett drove through the meadow, eventually coming up to the gate the girls had found. He shut the Gator off and waited for everyone to catch up. Brett helped the girls off the trailer and then had to again assist Snoop in getting down. Ava showed the adults the gate and described how they had cleaned off the vines, enabling them to climb over.

Now, the climb over for everyone was easy, except for Isabelle. She was handed over the gate from one adult to another.

Once on the other side, as the weeds and brush were almost as tall as Isabelle, Bryan decided to carry her on his shoulders until they found an area that was less overgrown where she could walk on her own. Riding atop her father's shoulders suited Isabelle just fine. Now, she again had an elevated spot with which to scan ahead for trouble.

Once everyone had gotten over the gate, Ava, Brooklyn, and Ellee began leading the way.

Looking back, Bryan said, "What's wrong with him?" pointing to Snoop, sitting by himself on the other side of the gate.

"He won't go under unless you coax him with some food," Ellee said

"Really! We'll see about that!" Brett said. Reaching under the bottom strand of barbed-wire, he simply pushed Snoop over on his side, then grabbed him by his front legs, forcefully dragging the dog under the fence. Once clear of the wire, Snoop stood up, as if nothing had happened.

Brett just shook his head and scolded the dog for his laziness. "Really, Snoop?" The girls just laughed and gave Snoop a thumbs-up. They knew what he was up to.

Pushing on, the girls stayed close to the creek, as they had done several days earlier. Before long, they spied the bright orange marker Ellee had tied in the sapling tree.

"That's the spot," Ava said, pointing up ahead to the marker. "We need to be really quiet from here on out," she instructed.

99

In just a matter of minutes, they came upon the log where they had sat the week before. Ava motioned to everyone that this was the place. Bryan put Isabelle down, and she crawled up on the log to sit with her sister and her two cousins. They were joined by Brett, Bryan, and Mr. Barry as well.

The researchers went quickly to work, quietly unpacking their equipment. Some took pictures of the flowers while others began taking pollen samples from the blooms. Mr. Martin and two of his assistants seemed to be discussing something important in hushed tones as they carefully examined the flowers.

One researcher took out a large pad of drawing paper and started making sketches of the flowers and the surrounding area. Isabelle, upon seeing this, immediately took a liking to this guy as well, and made a mental note to show him some of her sketches when they got back to the house.

Isabelle whispered to the man, pointing at the water, "Don't forget to sketch the pond. It's important." She had a serious look on her face.

The researcher glanced at the water, not understanding what the importance of the pond could possibly be to her, but nodded his head anyway. "Okay, I will," he whispered back to Isabelle.

The reporter from the local paper began snapping pictures of the area, as well as crowd shots of everyone there. He seemed to be very interested in everything that was going on.

Mr. Barry, sitting next to Brett and Bryan, began quietly telling the girls' fathers about a recent incident where he and some fellow officers had to chase some drug dealers through the woods. Mr. Barry told them that when they finally captured the criminals, the officers on scene discovered the cabin they had been hiding in was so contaminated from the drug making operations going on there, rather than trying to decontaminate the cabin, they just took a bulldozer, dug a big hole, knocked the house down, then simply pushed it into the hole and covered it with dirt.

Listening intently, Isabelle blurted out, "So you're like the Big Bad Wolf?" she asked, "knocking down houses."

Mr. Barry laughed. "Well sort of, but we were the good guys and they were the bad guys," he said, chuckling. "And as you know from the story," he explained, "the Big Bad Wolf was a bad guy. That's why they called him the Big *Bad* Wolf."

"Oh yeah… that's right!" Isabelle exclaimed. "If the Big Bad Wolf had a bulldozer, the last piggy in the brick house would have been smashed too!"

Mr. Barry just laughed.

"She's in preschool," Bryan said.

"I gathered as much," said Mr. Barry, chuckling again

While all this was going on, Mr. Holland, apparently with nothing to do, became bored. Looking around to the north, he spied the shed. "Anything up there in that shed?" he asked no one in particular. "Like tools and such?"

Immediately sensing an opportunity, Brooklyn spoke up, "Oh yeah. There's lots of stuff up there. Small farming tools and lots of old parts lying around," she said.

Ava had to put her hand over mouth to keep from laughing out loud.

"Well," Mr. Holland said, "while you are all waiting around here, I think I'll go up there and take a look around. Anybody have a problem with that?"

"Fine by us," the girls answered innocently.

Mr. Holland headed off in the direction of the shed. No one else even took notice of his leaving, as he walked off by himself. Ava leaned over and gave Brooklyn a high-five.

"Nice one, Brooklyn!" they all whispered, barely containing their laughter.

"Wouldn't it be righteous if *El Toro* was to suddenly show up!" whispered Ellee. This time the girls couldn't contain their laughter.

The researchers looked at the girls quizzically, wondering why the girls were now starting to act up. Brett and Bryan had to shush them.

Even though Ava was pretty sure 'El Toro' was not going to show up, her estimation of her sister's social skills and critical thinking had now just gone up dramatically.

Shortly after Mr. Holland disappeared, the girls heard a faint, familiar sound of buzzing wings. They signaled for everyone to be quiet and stay still. Everyone stopped what they were doing and listened intently.

All of a sudden, out of nowhere, a swarm of the strange looking insects descended on the flowers near the log where the girls were sitting. The researchers gawked in disbelief. All the men looked at Ava and she gave them her best, 'I told you so' smile.

Those with cameras still out began taking pictures. The researcher, who earlier had been making sketches of the flowers, began feverishly putting the insects to paper. Ava held out her hand to see what would happen, and just as before, one of the insects landed on her palm. Ava held her hand out toward the researchers so they could get a better look. They shook their heads in amazement.

"Is that him, Ava?" Isabelle asked.

"Of course it's him. See the pink dots? He's the only one with those," she said.

The researchers were excitedly but quietly discussing what to do next. One produced a small recording device, and holding it near the flowers, attempted to record the sounds the insects were making. Several researchers were already downloading some of the pictures to their laptops, hoping this would make identification faster.

Thinking the insects might disappear at any moment, the researchers worked quickly and efficiently, making sure not to harm the insects or damage the flowers. But the insects paid no attention whatsoever to the researchers. Eventually, the scientists decided they had collected enough data and most just sat back to watch and enjoy the show.

Brett took this opportunity to whisper to Mr. Martin, "Well, what do you think?"

Mr. Martin thought for a moment, choosing his words carefully, then said, "You know, I don't like to speculate, and of course we need to take our data back and have it all analyzed, but from what I've seen, I'd bet a dollar to a doughnut that these are something totally undiscovered. That is, of course, until last week," he added. "Everyone here seems to agree, but, like I said, we will have to wait until we get the results back from the data we've collected. What we can't figure out is just why no one has ever discovered them up until now."

Still thinking that over, Mr. Martin asked Brett, "You say the farmer who previously owned this property kept a bull up here in this area?"

"Yes he did. A very large one," said Brett. Lowering his voice, he added, "But he sold off all his livestock before we moved in."

"Well, it's just possible," Mr. Martin said, "the fact that he housed a bull up here probably kept most people out of this area."

"That would make sense," said Bryan. Just then, remembering something Mr. Gray had told them, Bryan added, "When we helped Mr. Gray round up his cattle, he told us that this farm had been in his family for generations, and as far as he knew, this was the area where the bulls were always kept."

"That might explain it then, why no one other than the owners ever set foot in here," said Mr. Martin. "It's quite possible these insects have been in here all that time, and no one ever saw them or just didn't pay any attention to them, that is, until your girls came along. Interesting."

Overhearing the conversation and not wanting to miss out on a good story, Mr. Koontz, the reporter from the local paper, said, "While the insects are still here, why don't we take some pictures of the girls sitting on the log with the insects and flowers in the background."

"That's a good idea," agreed Mr. Martin.

Getting the girls arranged on the log with Snoop at their feet, Mr. Koontz lined up the shot and took several pictures. He had Ava hold out her hand so the pictures would clearly show the one tiny creature still sitting on the palm of her hand.

Watching the photo shoot, Mr. Martin said, "If this turns out to be a new discovery, I am sure that Mr. Koontz will want to put an article in the local paper. You never know, the pictures might even go statewide or even national, with multi-media the way it is today," he added.

"I don't know if we're ready for all that," Bryan said.

Mr. Martin just smiled. The girls, however, were all nodding their heads, evidently agreeing with what Mr. Martin had just said.

The insects, however, still busy collecting nectar, did not seem to mind being 'discovered' or having their pictures taken, even though they very well might soon be introduced to the twenty-first century.

Chapter 23
What Goes Up…

Satisfied that he had taken enough pictures, Mr. Koontz said, "I hope Mr. Martin is right. This will make a great story!"

By now the group of researchers had begun packing up their equipment, putting notepads away, storing cameras and sensitive instruments, and securing all the samples they had collected.

All of a sudden they heard an inhuman scream coming from the direction of the shed. With everyone looking to the north, Mr. Holland appeared, running away from the shed toward the group, all the while screaming and flailing his arms about his face and body. As he reached the group of shocked onlookers, without breaking stride, he launched himself into mid-air, landing in the center of the shallow pool with a giant *ker-splash!* He immediately sank face first into the muck.

Having seen a similar dive on TV before during summer Olympic coverage, Ava calmly said to the other girls, "Too bad we don't have any scorecards to hold up. That dive was a perfect '10'."

"Yeah, and he stuck the landing," whispered Brooklyn.

The girls, like all good judges, stoically nodded their heads, then broke out into uncontrolled laughter.

With all the commotion now going on, no one bothered this time to quiet the girls down.

When Mr. Holland surfaced and was able to stand, he was completely covered in a thick layer of wet, sticky mud. He began attempting to wipe the muck from his eyes, nose, and mouth, with minimal success.

Producing a towel from a storage box located on the Gator, Brett tossed it to Mr. Holland. As he did his best to wipe the remaining muck from his face and arms, his bare skin was now showing a uniform patchwork of reddish welts that were visibly beginning to swell.

Ava leaned over and gave Brooklyn 'knuckles' once again. "Wow! Look at that!" was all she could say.

The Dragonpillar

Apparently, Mr. Holland, while rummaging around in the back of the shed, had disturbed a hornet's nest, and was now paying the price for his curiosity.

Ava whispered to Brooklyn, "Did you know those were in there?"

"Nope, didn't," Brooklyn replied, smiling.

Ellee, in her best clinical tone, now added, "Might have felt better if he had just left the mud on."

The girls started to giggle again.

"Ava!" Brett scolded, now turning his attention back to the girls.

All the girls now attempted, with little success, to hide their laughter by clamping their hands over their mouths.

The sudden noise had also startled the insects. Upon being rushed by a screaming madman, the swarm abruptly rose, momentarily hovering above the flowers, before flying off to the north. The last to leave was the one on Ava's hand. It rose up, flew a couple of times around Ava's head, then flew off to join its companions.

"Did you see that?" Mr. Gordon said in amazement. "It looked to me like it was tracing a... a halo, if you will, around her head."

"Yes, I saw that," said Mr. Martin. "That's most unusual. It's almost like that insect somehow recognizes her, but of course, that's impossible!" he exclaimed.

"Not to me it's not," said Ava. "He's special. He's my friend."

"Interesting," said all the researchers.

Mr. Martin then interjected, "You know, Ava, with those pink dots and that being the only insect we've seen so far marked like that, it's quite possible that that particular insect might be female. And if that's the case, I wouldn't at all be surprised if that particular insect isn't the queen, much like each hive of bees has a single queen bee."

Ava's mouth fell open in surprise at Mr. Martin's comments. She didn't quite know what to say. None of the girls had thought of that possibility.

"The Queen!" Ava said to herself. "I knew that one was special! In knew it!" Ava could barely contain her excitement.

With limited visibility restored, Mr. Holland now attempted to get out of the water, but found he couldn't budge. "Hey! I think I'm stuck!" he gasped.

"This is getting even better!" Brooklyn whispered to her sister. The girls continued to sit on the log, enjoying the show.

All the adults now balked at the idea of entering the water themselves in order to assist Mr. Holland. They momentarily milled around, not sure what to do next, no one wanting to make the first move.

The girls exchanged glances. Without speaking, they decided it was time to help out. Sliding off the log, Brooklyn simply said, "Rope."

Ava quickly added in a mock question to Ellee, "CPR?"

"Of course," Ellee said, getting her camera ready.

Brooklyn, Ava, and even Isabelle, began stretching out the rope still attached to the log, which up until now, no one else had noticed. In no visible hurry, Brett, Bryan, and Mr. Barry went to assist the girls with the rope rescue.

Stretching the rope to the water's edge, Brett coiled up the loose end, then tossed the rope to Mr. Holland. Although Mr. Holland caught the rope, due to the painful stings on his hands and arms, he was not able to pull himself out.

Mr. Barry then directed Mr. Holland to wrap the rope around his chest, just beneath his armpits. Once this was accomplished, Ellee got some excellent shots as they dragged Mr. Holland, moaning and groaning, through the mud and out onto the bank, minus his expensive Italian loafers.

Still holding her camera at the ready, Ellee looked back at Ava and gave her a thumbs-up. The girls began giggling again.

Upon seeing Mr. Holland finally on dry land, Ava proudly announced, "CPR has been accomplished!"

High-fives were exchanged amongst the girls. The rest of the adults tried not to laugh, but were not having much luck either.

Mr. Martin leaned over to Brett and Bryan. "Your girls are quite resourceful."

"Yes, I guess so," said Brett, not really knowing what to think.

"We think the word is *awesome!*" corrected Bryan. Mr. Martin nodded his head in agreement.

Mr. Barry immediately checked Mr. Holland's vital signs, taking his pulse and checking his breathing. Everything seemed to be within normal limits, at the moment, but Mr. Barry told the researchers that as soon as they got back to town, it would be a good idea to take him to the emergency room and have him evaluated before taking him home. They prepared to leave immediately.

Brooklyn now asked, "Ellee, you got any size 12 flip-flops in your backpack today?"

Ava and Ellee busted out laughing again. At this wisecrack, even Isabelle started giggling.

"Girls!" Brett and Bryan scolded. "That's enough!"

Because Mr. Holland was having some difficulty in walking, due to the multiple stings on his legs, he was piled onto the trailer for the trip back to the farmhouse.

Brett untied the rope from the log, coiled it up, and threw it on the trailer with Mr. Holland as well. "Nothing like a good piece of rope," he said, rubbing his hands together.

For some strange reason, all the girls, including Isabelle, decided to walk back, rather than ride on the trailer.

Before he pulled away, Brett once again saw Snoop sitting off to the side, eyeing the trailer. Getting out of his seat, he walked back to the dog. "You ready to get up there, Snoop?"

Taking a look at the lone occupant on the trailer, Snoop simply turned and started walking back to the house, falling in line behind the girls.

Chapter 24
When Life Gives You Lemons...

When the Gator pulled up to the farmhouse, Mr. Martin and the rest of his team helped Mr. Holland off the trailer. Mr. Barry once again checked his vital signs to make sure his breathing was not being compromised.

Upon seeing everyone return, Jill and Lee Ann brought out a large pitcher of lemonade and a second pitcher of ice, along with several empty glasses, all on a large tray.

Seeing Mr. Holland being off-loaded from the trailer and into the back of the car, Lee Ann asked if they needed to call an ambulance. Mr. Holland, in an irritated voice said, "No."

Instead of lemonade, Mr. Holland was handed through the back window of the car, several self-sealing plastic bags containing ice to apply to his swelling face.

Seeing her mother give only ice to Mr. Holland, Ellee whispered to the other girls, "Apparently the old saying that 'when life gives you lemons, you make lemonade', does not always work out in every situation."

Ellee got a stern look from her mother for that one.

Before Mr. Martin and his researchers left, they quickly thanked everyone for their hospitality and assistance. He said he would notify Mr. Gordon as soon as their analysis was complete, but it might take several weeks to make a formal announcement of their findings, due to the heavy workload they encounter at the university each spring.

Brooklyn, who had gone into the house, now came out with the vase of flowers, most still in fairly good condition. Holding the vase up, she said to Mr. Martin, "Maybe you can use some of these."

Recognizing the flowers, he said, "You bet! We didn't want to pick any of the flowers, but since you already have some, we can certainly use them!"

He carefully handed the vase to one of his assistants, who opened the trunk of the car and took out a special container which would preserve the flowers until they got them back to their lab. They handed the vase back to

Brooklyn, still containing some of the flowers, as they had only taken out a few for their research.

Catching everyone off-guard, Mr. Martin addressed the girls. "This is still premature, but have you thought of a name for these insects?" he asked. "If they turn out to be a new discovery, you girls will be credited with the discovery, and as such, will have the honor of naming them."

Brooklyn, Ellee, and Isabelle looked at Ava.

"Dragonpillars," Ava simply said. "They're Dragonpillars."

"Any particular reason?" Mr. Martin asked.

"Because," Ava said, "they sort of resemble a dragonfly, but they also look something like a caterpillar. So I just put the two together and came up with 'Dragonpillar.'"

The parents noticed Mr. Koontz diligently writing all this down, apparently for a newspaper article that he might get the opportunity to write later on.

"I like that, Ava," said Mr. Martin. He added, "What about the flowers? What if the flowers turn out to be a new discovery as well?"

The girls had a quick huddle, and Ellee and Isabelle could be seen nodding their heads in agreement to something Brooklyn was saying.

Finally, the huddle broke up, and Brooklyn excitedly announced, "We want them to be called 'Pink Bobbys'."

"Pink Bobbys?" Mr. Martin asked, puzzled. He could see the logic in Ava's name for the insects, but he was at a loss on 'Pink Bobbys'.

Brooklyn saw the puzzled look on his face. She quickly added, "Well… they just look just like something I have at home."

"Good enough for me," Mr. Martin said, chuckling. "Pink Bobbys it is!"

As the men piled into their car, Mr. Martin asked if it would be all right for them to come back at a later date to do more research. The girls' parents told them they were welcome to come back anytime and as many times as they liked. Mr. Barry also thanked them as well, before leaving.

As they drove off, Ava was thinking to herself that it had been a long time since she was actually looking forward to sitting at her desk during homeroom.

As the cars disappeared down the road, an idea popped into Brooklyn's head and excitedly she said, "I got it, Ava! I know what you can use for your project! Maybe you can catch a hornet to turn in!"

The other three girls just stood there with blank stares on their faces.

Suddenly Ava began to think that her earlier assessment of her sister's critical thinking might have been a little premature. With Brooklyn's last statement, sadly, Ava's assessment was now starting to go back down.

"I don't think that's such a good idea, Brooklyn," Ava said, patting her sister on the back.

"Well," said Brooklyn, "it *was* just an idea."

Mr. Martin and his fellow researchers took Mr. Holland to the emergency room, as suggested, to get checked out before taking him home.

Sitting in one of those emergency room cubicles, a nurse came in to examine Mr. Holland. "What on earth have you been into?" she asked in surprise, seeing all the welts on his face, neck, and arms.

One of the assistants tried to explain. "We were out at the old Farmer Gray property, doing some research, and he evidently ran into some hornets."

Giving Mr. Holland a shot, just as a precaution to control the swelling, the ER nurse commented, "Research, huh?"

Now trying to 'inject' a little emergency room humor into an otherwise uncomfortable situation, she said, "You look a little too old to be taking part in *cow tipping*."

The researchers had been told the cow tipping story earlier that day, and now were again all trying to hide a chuckle. Mr. Holland, however, was not amused.

Apparently this nurse had been working a Friday night shift a couple of years ago during the month of October.

On Monday, Mr. Holland showed up for work at school, apparently no worse for wear, as most of the swelling had gone down and the red welts had become less visible. However, it was reported that several male students received after-school detention that day for repeatedly making loud 'buzzing' noises while walking past Mr. Holland's open classroom door.

Chapter 25
Adults!

The next day, Bryan showed up at the farmhouse around one p.m., with Ellee and Isabelle in tow. Brett wanted to start taking down the fence earlier in the morning, but Bryan, Lee Ann, and the girls had gone to church and didn't get home until noon.

Brett went into the barn, once again pulling out the Gator. After hooking up the trailer and loading some tools and gloves, they loaded up the girls and Snoop, minus Ava. She was still grounded for one more day, and therefore, couldn't go along.

However Ava didn't gripe about it. As her father had several pairs of binoculars, she decided to keep tabs on what they were doing, much the same way as Isabelle had done earlier.

As they pulled away, Brooklyn gave Ava a thumbs-up. Brooklyn had loaded her butterfly net on the trailer, just in case. Isabelle had her pair of binoculars and was apparently still in lookout mode, although at this point it wasn't really necessary. Brett and Bryan could see, however, that she was still really enjoying herself, so no one told her otherwise.

As they headed up into the meadow, the afternoon was already heating up. Nearing the barbed-wire fence, Bryan said, "Why don't we just take down this one section of fence? It's already getting hot, and that will be a lot less work. We can take the rest down at a later date, maybe when it's not as hot and we have more time."

'That's what I was thinking, too," said Brett. "Too bad we didn't have time to do this before yesterday, but after today, no one will have to climb that gate anymore."

"Or we could just cut the chain off and open the gate," Ellee added.

Brett and Bryan just looked at each other.

They parked the Gator close to the fence and unloaded the girls and Snoop. Seeing that the weeds in this area were still quite tall, Isabelle decided to set up her 'command post' right where she sat, on the trailer.

As Brett and Bryan unloaded their tools, Brooklyn was eyeing the shed up to the north. Ellee could sense that Brooklyn was reliving her adventure from the week before.

Instead of climbing the gate, the girls decided to search the general area on the side of the fence they were already on and wait for their parents to take down enough of the barbed-wire so they could just walk through. Besides, they wanted Snoop to go along and they didn't bring any food this time with which to coax him under the fence.

Brooklyn picked up her butterfly net, and Ellee shouldered her pink backpack. From the vantage point of the trailer, Isabelle was already scanning the area, again performing her duties flawlessly.

"Think about it," Ellee said to Brooklyn, as they watched their fathers start to dismantle the fence. "If my dad and your dad are taking down this fence, doesn't that tell you that the bull isn't up here anymore?"

Brooklyn, acting like she had already figured that out as well, said with a nod, "Yeah, that's what I was thinking, too."

Brett and Bryan began carefully cutting the strands of barbed-wire along the nearest gatepost, one at a time. As they cut each strand, they would roll it up, away from the gate, toward the next fencepost down the line.

As they cut the last strand attached to the gatepost, the path was now clear, and Brooklyn and Ellee simply walked through. For some reason, merely walking through did not seem nearly as exciting to both girls as climbing the gate had been the week before.

"Well, that was easy," commented Ellee.

"If Ava were here she would say, 'Easy-peasy, lemon-squeezy!'" Brooklyn said. Both girls laughed.

"We're going to go look around in here now," Brooklyn said to her father.

"All right," said Brett, "but stay out of the creek and it would be a good idea to stay out of that shed as well. We haven't had the chance to get rid of the hornets yet."

"Really!" both girls said, giving him their best look of exasperation.

"Well... err," Brett stammered, "I guess you already knew that."

Shaking their heads, Brooklyn, Ellee, and Snoop trudged off. When they were out of earshot, Brooklyn exclaimed, "Adults!"

"Yeah," said Ellee. "They must think we have a really short memory, but they are sort of handy to have around!"

When the girls and Snoop got back to the Gator, several large rolls of neatly coiled barbed-wire were stacked on the flatbed trailer. Afraid Isabelle might get cut on the wire, the 'command post' had been moved to the backseat of the vehicle. Ellee and Brooklyn squeezed onto the back seat as well, and Snoop was sandwiched on the floorboard, between feet and legs, for the ride back.

When they arrived back at the farmhouse, everyone got off, but the coils of wire were left on the trailer. "We'll get Dad to come by with his truck and take all this stuff to the recycling center," Brett said.

"I'm glad we at least got a section done today."

"Yep, me too," said Bryan, as they all headed into the farmhouse to get something cold to drink.

Bryan carefully picked up Isabelle, still clutching the binoculars. She had fallen asleep in the seat on the way back. Carrying her into the house, he said laughing, "Today's 'tour of duty' just must have been too much for her. Should we tell her when she wakes up that soldiers get shot for falling asleep while on guard duty?"

"That's probably not a good idea," said Brett.

"Yeah, probably not," agreed Bryan.

Brooklyn and Ellee simply rolled their eyes at the comment. "Adults!" they whispered to each other, as their fathers entered the house ahead of them.

Chapter 26
The Verdict is In

The weather forecast for the coming week was again for warm temperatures and drier conditions than normal for that time of year.

Ava had served her time and was no longer grounded. However, after school that week, as she had seen on her softball schedule, she had travel team softball practice on Monday and Wednesday after school, and league games on Tuesday and Thursday evenings at Lassie League Park in town. Then on Saturday, her travel team was participating in their first tournament of the spring, and it was out of town. With the deadline for turning in a specimen for her class project on the following Monday, that meant she only had a couple of days left to look for a specimen. However, she was determined not to give up.

After her softball game on Tuesday evening, as Brett pulled up to the house with Ava, she noticed Bryan and Lee Ann's car parked in front of their house. As they walked in, everyone was sitting in the living room. The television was not on. Something did not feel quite right to Ava. She looked at Brooklyn and Ellee and they both slightly shrugged their shoulders, indicating to her that they didn't know what was going on either. Ava was instructed to get herself something to drink, then come and sit with the other girls.

By the time Ava re-entered the living room, she was pretty sure that the rest of their punishment was about to be announced, in one form or the other. She took a seat, but for some reason, their parents continued to chit-chat about nothing in particular. The girls kept shooting each other puzzled looks, and one by one, it began to dawn on the other three what was about to transpire. However, even as the girls went silent, again, nothing was brought up about punishment.

At about that time, Ava heard a car pull into the driveway, and then momentarily there was a loud knock on the door. It made the girls jump.

Brett answered the door, greeting an older gentleman by saying, "Please come in and have a seat."

The man who entered the house was much older than their parents. His hair was graying at the temples and he wore reddish, wire-rimmed glasses. Ironically, it seemed he was wearing almost the same type of 'uniform' as had most everyone else who had visited the house in the last several weeks; a khaki short-sleeved shirt with official-looking patches sewn on the sleeves, and khaki trousers, although this gentleman was carrying a rather large briefcase, which he set down on the table in front of him.

Ava had no idea who he was or what he was doing there, but her general impression of the man was that he was friendly. Brooklyn, on the other hand, was sure they were now all going to be inducted into some type of scouting organization. Ellee, who was intently studying the man, had not yet come to any conclusions.

Isabelle, however, although not seeing a gun, was sure the man was a police officer, and was sure their parents had turned them all in to law enforcement. They were all going to be sent to jail, for an unspecified period of time, for rehabilitation.

With her bright blue eyes, she just glared at the man. She had seen just this sort of thing on television before, and knew it would go easier on her if she showed no sign of weakness, especially later, when the prison population began screaming at her.

However, rather than reading them their rights and taking them off to jail, the man sitting in front of them simply introduced himself as Mr. Nelson, one of the agriculture teachers at the high school and also the 4-H youth project coordinator for the county, which included organizing and overseeing youth projects and exhibits for the county fair. The girls sensed that their parents already knew this man.

The girls just sat there, not yet knowing what to think. However, for some reason, Snoop had gone over to Mr. Nelson and was snuggling up to his leg.

Noticing Snoop's reaction to Mr. Nelson, Ava thought to herself, *Snoop's a pretty good judge of character, so this guy must be all right.*

At this point, Mr. Nelson explained the reason for his visit. "I received a call the other day from a Mr. Martin at Purdue University. He sent me some interesting pictures he said one of you girls had taken on your farm. He asked me if I knew anything about it, and I told him 'no'. He then asked me if I would check it out for myself."

Continuing, he said, "He knew our county fair was coming up in less than two months and a lot of people might be interested in what you girls found. We are always looking for new and exciting projects and exhibits for our youth to work on, and he said that with the information you had already collected, if you girls agree to, that is, you could put together a very interesting exhibit that a lot of people attending the fair would enjoy seeing."

The girls started to visibly relax. Ellee leaned over to Ava and whispered, "If this is somehow related to our punishment, count me in."

Ava nodded. Whispering back, she said, "Let's just see what else he has to say."

'I understand," Mr. Nelson continued, "that besides a lot of photographs, you have some wonderful sketches of your adventure as well."

The other three girls looked at Isabelle, and nodded. Isabelle was now starting to loosen up as well, realizing that she was probably not going to wind up like the 'Birdman of Alcatraz' after all.

"I also understand that you collected some very unusual flowers," Mr. Nelson added.

"Yeah, Pink Bobbys!" Brooklyn nearly shouted out. "Daddy showed me how to save them. We dried and pressed them in a large book, and they still look like new, just a little flatter now though!"

"Very good," said Mr. Nelson, approvingly. "Well," he continued, "if you were to take all your materials and write up a story about how you discovered all this, I think it would make for a very interesting exhibit for the fair. However, it will require a lot of work, and the fair starts, let's see, yes, the fair starts on June 20. All projects and exhibits have to be at the fairgrounds one week before the fair actually starts, so that means that your project would have to be completed and delivered there by the 13th. That still gives you at least a full six weeks to complete your project, which should be plenty of time to get everything put together. What do you think?" he finally asked, looking at the girls.

The girls began talking in hushed tones amongst themselves.

At this point, Mr. Nelson decided to chat briefly with the parents and let the girls consider his proposal. Mr. Nelson began scratching Snoop's ears.

"I think he likes you," Jill said.

"I believe so," Mr. Nelson chuckled. "What breed of dog is he?"

"Beagle, of course," Brett said. "We call him the world's *largest* beagle."

"Oh!" Mr. Nelson said in surprise. Examining Snoop more closely, Mr. Nelson said, "He might very well be the world's largest beagle!" Everyone laughed.

Besides Snoop, the girls were really starting to like Mr. Nelson. His soft-spoken manner and his genuine interest in the girls was beginning to win them over.

Mr. Nelson looked at his watch. "Well, I really do need to be going. I have to meet with some other youths about their projects." To the girls he said, "Why don't you have your parents call me if you decide to do the exhibit."

The girls looked at their parents, but the parents were not giving any indication either way of what they thought the girls should do. From this, Ava surmised that there might be other options for punishment, less humane, so to speak, if they decided against doing the project. However, Ava was truly interested in Mr. Nelson's proposal and thought the idea of creating an exhibit about their discoveries would be a lot of fun.

Brooklyn was thinking it was way better than being indoctrinated into a scouting organization and being made to go door to door, trying to sell expensive cookies, although there is actually nothing wrong with joining a scouting organization and being involved in fundraisers. It's just not what she was interested in at the moment.

Isabelle was sure it was way better than doing hard time.

Ellee, on the other hand, was already thinking of the best way to format her pictures and organize all their material for the exhibit, for maximum public appeal, of course.

"Don't need to call," Ava said to Mr. Nelson. "I'm in."

"I'm in too," said Brooklyn.

"Me three," said Isabelle, smiling. All the parents chuckled.

"What about you, Ellee?" her mother Lee Ann asked.

"Oh! Oh!" said Ellee, her train of thought broken by the unexpected question. "I was in the minute Snoop gave you his stamp of approval," she said to Mr. Nelson. They all laughed again, with all the girls crowding around Snoop, scratching his ears and patting him on the back.

"Well, I guess that's settled then," Mr. Nelson said.

Before he left, he told the girls he would be providing them with an official entry form in the next few days as well as additional information they would be needing about the entry process. As he left, he thanked everyone sincerely for their time and attention in listening to his proposal.

"I can't wait to see your finished exhibit," he told the girls as he walked out the door.

"Oh, by the way," he added, speaking to the parents in a hushed tone. "You might want to keep a sharp eye on the local paper in the next few days. I have a feeling there might be something in there that will interest you," he said with a wink. He left with no further explanation.

As his car pulled away, Bryan said, "I wonder what that was all about?"

"Not sure," said Brett, "but I guess we'll find out soon enough."

Before Ellee and Isabelle went home that evening, all four girls were already upstairs in Ava and Brooklyn's bedroom, going over their materials and coming up with ideas on how best to put their exhibit together.

The girls were feeling pretty good about the way the evening had turned out.

"Maybe adults aren't so bad after all," Brooklyn said. The other girls just nodded their heads, apparently agreeing.

Chapter 27
Do Unto Others…

That week, the weather forecast turned out to be accurate. In the afternoons, the temperatures rose to the mid-80s and no rain fell at all.

The girls stayed busy with school activities and worked on their fair project as time allowed. Mr. Nelson stopped by on Friday and dropped off an official entry form for their exhibit, as well some material that gave suggestions on how to put an exhibit together, complete with examples of past projects that had been entered. He also informed them that when the fair was over, all projects and exhibits had to be picked up during the day no later than the following Saturday. Otherwise, items left in the exhibit buildings would become the property of the fair board, and would probably be thrown away. Mr. Nelson gave their parents a phone number for the fairgrounds office so they could call ahead and make sure the exhibit buildings were open before driving over to pick up their project.

While Mr. Nelson was at the house, he asked the girls how the exhibit was going. Ava let Mr. Nelson read part of what she had written so far about their adventure. He said it sounded great, and thought they were all doing an excellent job so far and encouraged them to keep up the good work.

Brooklyn showed Mr. Nelson a large, matted picture frame that her mother had purchased. It was specifically designed to hold and display dried flowers. The frame could be stood up independently on a table for public viewing without having to be hung up.

After several attempts, Brooklyn had meticulously mounted her dried 'Pink Bobbys' in the frame, and then had carefully replaced the glass.

Showing the mounted flowers to Mr. Nelson, he was impressed. He said they looked professionally mounted. Brooklyn just beamed with pride at his remarks.

The next day, Saturday, Ava and Brooklyn didn't get home until late that night. Ava had been participating in her first softball tournament out of town and all the family had attended.

On Sunday, after church, Ava and Brooklyn decided to take one last trip over to the meadow, to see if they could finally find something for Ava to turn in for her class project. The deadline for turning something in was the next day.

It had been exactly a full week since anyone had been over to the meadow, and with the unusually hot and dry week it had been, Ava was not sure if they would see anything at all. Bryan had come over with Ellee, but Lee Ann had taken Isabelle to a birthday party being held for one of Isabelle's preschool classmates.

"Darn! What are we going to do? No lookout today!" Ava said.

"I know. I'm worried," Ellee said laughing.

Brett and Bryan decided to work on a project in the barn and told the girls they would have to walk, as they were not going either.

"What are you guys working on in the barn?" asked Ava.

"Mmmm… something," said her father.

"Like what kind of something?" Brooklyn asked, looking puzzled.

"Well," their father stalled, "it's sort of like a surprise, maybe, if we get it done," he said, looking at Bryan.

"Come on," Ava whispered to Ellee and Brooklyn. "When they leave, we'll sneak around in the barn to see what they were working on. We'll find out what the big secret is!" The girls all giggled, nodding their heads.

"Maybe we should wait for Isabelle!" said Brooklyn. "She could keep an eye on them while we are snooping around in there!"

"Oh not again!" Ellee said. They all began giggling.

The girls took off walking toward the meadow. Ava and Brooklyn took along their butterfly nets, which by now, were starting to show some signs of wear and tear. Of course, Ellee was taking her pink backpack along.

"My mom thinks I'm a hoarder," Ellee said, motioning to her overstuffed backpack. "What do you guys think?"

"Nah!" said her cousins. "Everything in there comes in handy at one time or another," they said.

Ellee broke out in a huge grin, obviously agreeing with their answer.

The Dragonpillar

Once in the meadow, they decided to search a few areas they hadn't searched in a while, but since the day was already heating up, few insects seemed to be out and moving about.

Ava stopped briefly to tie up her long, brown hair. Reaching in her pocket, she pulled out several colored ribbons. She selected her favorite color, pink, and stuffed the rest back into her pocket.

Having tied her hair back into a ponytail, she said to herself, "That feels much cooler!"

Before they left the house, Brooklyn had already tied her straight, long, blonde hair up in pigtails. For some reason, she preferred pigtails to ponytails.

Ellee, on the other hand, didn't really need to tie her hair up in any configuration. Even at age nine, her platinum blonde hair was so curly, that Bryan and Lee Ann worried that it would never reach her shoulders. Visions of Albert Einstein haunted her parents.

Having searched for some time and not found anything, the girls decided to go back to the creek and follow it up to the log where they had first discovered the Dragonpillars.

Nearing the area, Ava spotted the orange marker in the tree, then the log and all the flowers came into view. In some way, something seemed different to Ava. It did not seem quite as exciting as it all had been the first few times they had been there, but rather than saying so, she decided to keep this feeling to herself.

They sat down on the log to rest a bit, with Ellee removing her backpack and setting it on the ground at her feet as before. All of a sudden Brooklyn screamed, startling both girls.

Ava and Ellee began frantically looking around, thinking the insects had returned, or something much worse. Maybe the bull had shown up after all. But they didn't see anything. They couldn't see any reason why Brooklyn was screaming.

Brooklyn, with her mouth open in shock, was pointing in the direction of the pond. "Ava, look!" she screamed! "Something's happened to the pond!"

In amazement, they all looked in that direction, trying to comprehend what they saw.

Somehow, the shallow pond where Ava had been stuck had completely dried up, revealing the clay bottom. It was now baked hard by the week's sunshine and lack of rain, and no more than ten feet from where the water's edge had been, Ava's shoes lay sticking out of the dried mud.

"What... what happened?" stammered Ava.

"That's impossible!" exclaimed Brooklyn.

Thinking out loud, Ellee said, "This is really weird. What's going on here?"

"Remember," Ava said to the other two, "on the way up here we followed the creek, and the water was still flowing, right?"

"Yeah, that's right," said Ellee, puzzled. "How is that possible if the pond is dry? That's really strange!"

Looking out over the clay bottom, Ava exclaimed, "But I'm not complaining. I think I can reach my shoes now!"

The girls stood gawking a little while longer, still not fully comprehending what had happened to the pond. It just didn't make any sense.

Finally, Ellee, who had been studying something across the pond on the opposite bank said, "Hey! What's that over there?"

Looking across the pond to where Ellee was pointing, Ava, with a puzzled look on her face, said as well, "What is that over there?"

"Beats me," said Brooklyn, scratching her head.

The girls were now looking at the spot where the creek had originally emptied into the pond from the north. A small dike, apparently made of mud, small twigs, and leaves, was blocking the water and keeping it from entering the now dry pond.

"Where'd that thing come from?" asked Brooklyn. "Where's the water going?"

"Look!" exclaimed Ellee. "The water's being diverted around the far side of the pond. See that little wall over there?" she said, pointing. "It extends from that dike thing on this end and runs all the way around the far bank where the pond used to be, then the wall curves back down to there," she said, pointing to where the creek starts up again, on the south end of the pond.

"That's why we saw water still flowing in the lower part of the creek on the way up here," Ava said. "The water is just going around the pond, allowing it to dry up. That's unbelievable!"

"Seems so," said Ellee. "That's really strange!"

"I... I just can't believe this!" exclaimed Ava. "Who in the world would have done this and for what reason?

"I have no idea, Ava," said Brooklyn.

"No one's going to believe this!" said Ellee, shaking her head.

Finally, Ava, overcoming her shock, came to a decision. "Just in case," she said, looking at Brooklyn and Ellee as she removed her shoes. They nodded, now realizing what Ava was getting ready to do.

"Looks solid enough to me," Ava said, as she gingerly stepped off the bank onto the baked clay. The clay seemed to support her weight.

Before she had taken two steps, Ellee yelled, "Wait!" Ellee handed Ava her camera.

"Take some pictures," she said.

"Good idea," Ava said.

Balancing herself, Ava turned and continued across. In just a few short strides, she reached her shoes. Bending down, she tried to pull her shoes free, but they resisted. Pulling harder, the clay finally gave up its grip and her shoes broke free. She tossed them up on the bank toward Brooklyn and Ellee.

Satisfied, she turned and crossed the remaining distance to the far side. What she saw simply amazed her. "This thing is an engineering marvel! I bet those guys from Purdue would even be impressed with this construction!"

The tiny wall, no more than fifteen inches high, was made of tightly compacted mud containing twigs and leaves for additional strength. And just as Ellee had suspected, the dike indeed was diverting the water from the creek, around the outer edge of this wall, then allowing the water to flow back into the creek on the south end of the pond.

From where she stood, Ava could easily see the water flowing on the other side of the wall. Turning Ellee's camera on, she took multiple pictures of everything.

"It's really amazing!" she exclaimed, shouting back to Brooklyn and Ellee.

Satisfied that she had taken enough pictures, Ava turned around and again, gingerly started on her way back across the clay bottom.

Nearing the two holes in the mud where her shoes had been, she spied something else barely sticking out of the mud. Reaching down to investigate, she exclaimed, "No way!"

"What is it?" the other two girls shouted!

"You're not going to believe this either," Ava said, as she pulled something else out of the dried mud.

"Try us," they both said at the same time.

"It's Mr. Holland's shoes!" she proudly proclaimed, as she held up one muddy Italian loafer for Brooklyn and Ellee to see.

They all started laughing. Ava pinched her nose as if smelling something awful.

"Leave 'em!" said Brooklyn. They all laughed again.

Ava paused briefly, thinking, then bent back down and pulled out the mate to the shoe. Getting close to the bank, she tossed them up on the grass as well.

"You gonna give those back to him?" asked Ellee.

"Well," Ava said, "I'm going to clean them up first, then we'll see. I'd want somebody to do that for me," she added. "If they're not ruined, yeah, I'll give them back."

From her backpack, Ellee produced a large plastic bag for Ava to put the shoes in. The girls decided to sit on the log a little while longer, now remembering the reason why they were there in the first place. Ellee and Brooklyn began scanning through the pictures Ava had just taken.

"These pictures really are amazing," Ellee said. "I have no idea who or what could have built that," she said.

"Do you think beavers could have done it?" asked Brooklyn.

"That's the only thing I can think of," said Ellee, "but I really doubt it. Beavers cut down small trees and pile them up in round-looking 'huts', but I don't think they make anything this small and detailed," she added.

Ava said, "It sort of reminds me the way a robin builds its nest or maybe like some wasps do, 'mud dabbers', I think they're called. They make their small homes entirely out of mud."

The girls were discussing other possibilities, when an insect, out of nowhere, landed on one of Ava's muddy tennis shoes. "It's her!" Ava exclaimed. "What's she doing?"

The Dragonpillar

In a matter of minutes, Ava's shoes were nearly covered by the insects, coming and going. This time, for some reason, they were completely ignoring the flowers.

As the girls watched this strange behavior, Ava said, "Guys, I might be crazy, but it looks to me like they are trying to clean my shoes off! Look! See? There goes one now, and it's carrying off a tiny piece of mud from one of my shoes!"

The girls watched in amazement. When Ava looked up, Ellee was nodding at her as if she had just come to some extraordinary conclusion.

Staring out over the pond at the dike, Ellee said, "Ava, you don't think... " her voice now trailing off in thought. The implication of what Ellee was considering hit Ava as well.

"No way! Impossible!" exclaimed Ava.

"Well," Ellee said, "unless you have a better explanation... " her voice trailing off again, not needing to finish the sentence.

The girls just looked at the insects, then at the dike, then back at the insects. It was just too impossible to really be true, but no one could come up with any other plausible explanation.

Ellee took a few pictures of Ava's tennis shoes covered with the insects, then stored her camera.

Ava had seen enough for one day and was ready to go back, even though she hadn't found a specimen to turn in. She carefully picked up her tennis shoes. The insects scattered, flying off to the north as before, but not before the one sporting the pink dots landed on Ava's hand. It blinked its eyes at Ava, then abruptly rose up and again flew a circle around her, before disappearing.

"What do you make of that?" Ava asked Ellee. "That's the second time she has done that!"

"Ava," Ellee said, "I really don't know, but at this point, I'd believe almost anything!"

On the way back, the girls decided to keep their latest discovery a secret, at least for now. Ava knew, from playing cards with her father, that there was value in 'not laying all your cards on the table at the one time'. Maybe they would tell the scientists at some point, maybe not. She also wanted to clean up her new shoes and see how long it took for her parents to notice that she had them back.

As they approached the back door, Brooklyn wondered out loud, "I wonder where Snoop was today?"

"Tonight is Daddy's birthday, and I think Mommy was going to bake him a special treat," Ava said. "Snoop probably hung around the kitchen all day, waiting."

Ava and Brooklyn laughed. Ellee just shook her head.

Before she walked in the back door, Ava washed the mud off both pairs of shoes with the garden hose.

Knowing how her leather ball glove would shrink after getting wet, after she washed off Mr. Holland's leather shoes, she wadded up some newspaper and packed it into the toes so they wouldn't shrink too badly. She then hid his shoes behind a flower pot on the 'deck-porch' to air dry.

Satisfied with her efforts, she quietly took her tennis shoes into the laundry room and threw them in the washer with a load of dirty towels.

Ava noticed then that Snoop had not been at the back door to greet them. *That's odd*, she thought to herself. Before turning on the washer, she yelled, "Okay if I do some towels?"

"Sure, thanks, Ava," Jill yelled back.

"At least something was going right!" Jill murmured to herself.

Walking into the kitchen, the girls noticed Snoop lying on his back, asleep under the kitchen table, and they could tell their mother was not in a very good mood.

Chapter 28
Leap of Faith

"What's Snoop doing sleeping under the kitchen table?" Ava asked her mother. Brooklyn bent down under the table to scratch his belly.

"His tummy's making 'gurgling noises," Brooklyn said to Jill, "and his belly looks extra big!"

Ava got under the table to check Snoop out for herself. "Wow!" she exclaimed, "what's he been eating?"

"Don't bother Snoop," their mother said rather angrily. "I'm mad at him!"

Drying a medium-sized cake pan she had just washed with a hand towel, Jill turned to the girls and said, "Your father said he'd rather have brownies than a cake for his birthday tonight, so I made a special trip into town to get brownie mix while you girls were over in the meadow. After I took the brownies out of the oven, I set them up here on the counter to cool, then I went out to hang up some laundry on the line."

Uh-oh! Ava thought to herself, looking down at her dog.

"I was only out there for a few minutes," Jill said. "When I came back in, Snoop was up on the counter, leaning over the pan, cleaning up the last few crumbs of your father's brownies!"

"Whoa!" said Ava, now looking at Snoop's recently enhanced girth.

"He ate an entire 9 by 13 inch pan of brownies in a matter of minutes! I'm not talking to him!" she added angrily, turning back to the kitchen sink.

Looking at Snoop lying between the legs of the kitchen table, Brooklyn said laughing, "Did you do that, Snoop?"

Ava and Ellee knew better than to laugh, but were again having difficulty keeping it in. They rarely saw Jill this mad. Laughter in many situations can be a good stress reliever, but in this case, they wisely decided to keep quiet, as Jill continued banging pots and pans on the kitchen countertop.

Turning around again, Jill pointed her finger at the dog and exclaimed, *"Bad Snoop!"*

Brett and Bryan, apparently having finished working in the barn on their secret project, were coming in the back door as Jill was chastising the dog.

Coming into the kitchen, Brett said, "What's going on?"

Jill didn't respond.

"Guess what?" Ava said to her father, sounding a little too proud.

Angrily, Jill whirled around and said to Brett, "Yeah, guess what *your* dog did?"

Before answering, it occurred to Brett that as long as Snoop was cute, loveable, and did funny stuff, he was everyone's dog. However, when he did something bad, he somehow always turned into *his* dog.

However, judging Jill's present state of irritation, Brett decided now was not the time to pursue that topic. Instead, he simply asked, "What did he do?"

Ava and Brooklyn had to fill him in on the details as Jill had gone 'mum'.

Ellee, who had been listening intently to the conversation, leaned over to Ava and whispered, "I guess Snoop didn't need to figure out a way to get that oven door open after all."

Ava and Brooklyn couldn't help but giggle out loud. Jill was not amused.

Brett went over to Jill and tried to smooth things over. "You know," he said, "it's okay. I really appreciate all the trouble you went through to fix me brownies, but really, it's all right."

Jill, sniffling a little, turned and asked, "How do you think he got up there anyway?" She pointed to the countertop.

Looking down at the dog, Brett said, "Well, you can bet he didn't jump up there!"

"When I came in," Jill said, "he was too scared to jump down even though he knew he was caught and was in big trouble. I had to physically pick him up and set him down on the floor. As soon as I put him down, he ran over to his water bowl, which I had just filled up, and drank it dry!"

"I'd be thirsty too if I had just eaten that many brownies!" Brooklyn said matter-of-factly.

Brooklyn got a stern look from her father. Ava and Ellee, under the kitchen table, were again trying to stifle their laughter by clamping their hands over their mouths, but somehow the laughs just seemed to squeeze out between their fingers.

With Jill's question still unanswered, everyone began examining the layout of the kitchen. No one could come up with a reasonable explanation of how Snoop had gotten up on the countertop.

Finally, Bryan, who had been sitting quietly drinking a cold soda said, "I would say the only way he could have done it would have been to get up on a kitchen chair, climb up on the kitchen table, then jump over onto the countertop."

Brett, trying to figure out if this feat was even possible, took a tape measure out of the top kitchen drawer. Measuring the distance between the countertop and the closest side of the kitchen table, he announced the distance to be a whopping six feet.

Scratching his head, he said, "Wow, I don't know. That's quite a leap, especially when you take into consideration that he would have been taking off from the slick tabletop, and when he landed, he wouldn't have had any room to slow down before crashing into the cabinet doors!"

Now the attention turned back to Snoop.

Ava, sitting under the table next to Snoop asked, "Daddy, do you think he's going to be all right?"

Brett crawled under the table to check on *his* dog. Checking Snoop out, he said, "I don't know, Ava. He's sleeping right now, but maybe we should call the vet."

Ellee then added, "Uncle Brett, you know, chocolate is bad for dogs."

Brett just shook his head. "It's a little too late for that now, don't you think, Doctor Ellee?" Brett said. She simply nodded in agreement.

Brett started to crawl out from under the table in order to call the vet's office, when Jill confessed. "I already called them. The vet said unless he gets really hyper, or starts acting strangely, or starts throwing up a lot, he'll probably be all right. They said not to move him, just let him sleep it off."

"He doesn't look too hyper at the moment to me, Uncle Brett," Ellee added one more time in her best clinical tone.

"Why, thank you, Doctor Ellee, for your quick diagnosis," Brett said, somewhat amused at watching his niece, as she was now holding Snoop's paw between her thumb and index finger, apparently trying to take his pulse.

Brett just looked at her, not knowing what to say next. "I'm not sure it works that way," he said with a chuckle to Ellee. "By chance, do you watch a lot of doctor shows on television?"

"Just trying to help, Uncle Brett," she said smiling, tenderly putting Snoop's paw down.

"Yes, I see," said Brett.

"How do you know he's sleeping, Daddy?" Ava asked her father.

"Look," Brett said, pointing to the dog. "He's running in his sleep. See how his eyes seem to be darting back and forth under his eyelids and how his front paws look like they're 'dog-paddling' in mid-air? He's chasing something in his sleep."

"Really?" all the girls asked.

As the girls got up even closer to Snoop, in order to see what Brett was talking about, Snoop started softly growling. The girls all giggled.

"What do you think he's chasing?" Brooklyn asked her father.

"Probably rabbits, if I had to guess," Brett said.

"Probably more like chocolate bunnies!" Jill exclaimed. This time, even Jill had to laugh at her own joke.

Before going to bed, Ava took her tennis shoes out of the washer, threw the towels in the dryer, then turned it on. After untangling the shoelaces, she set the shoes out back on the 'deck-porch' to air dry, next to Mr. Holland's expensive Italian loafers.

Coming back inside, she immediately went to bed, but not before checking on Snoop. He hadn't budged. He was still asleep under the kitchen table, on his back, snoring.

During the night, Brett got up and checked on Snoop as well. Secretly, even Jill got up a couple of times herself to check on the dog. Apparently she had gotten over the theft of her brownies.

In the morning, as Brett was getting ready to go to work, he went into the kitchen to start some coffee. Snoop was sitting patiently at the back door, waiting for someone to let him out.

"Well," Brett said to the dog, "you're looking no worse for wear," as he opened the back door to let him out.

The Dragonpillar

Snoop made a beeline for the barn, disappearing around the far corner. A few minutes later he reappeared, walking back up to the house, his morning 'business' evidently finished.

About mid-way to the house, he froze in his tracks. Looking in the direction of the chicken coops, he spied a couple of the feathered freeloaders scratching and pecking their way around in the yard.

Sipping his coffee and looking out the window, Brett decided to watch and see what would happen next. Brett imagined that Snoop was probably trying to figure out a way to run down one of those chickens. In just a matter of seconds though, Snoop turned and resumed his walk back to the house.

"Guess not," Brett said to himself.

When Snoop got to the back door, Brett opened it and let the dog in. "Enough exercise for today?" Brett asked the dog. "Snoop, we're simply gonna have to get you on that diet!"

Ignoring what his master was saying, Snoop simply walked through the kitchen and headed for the living room couch for a well-deserved, early morning nap. By the time Brett was ready to leave for work, Snoop was already curled up in a ball on the couch, snoring, as usual.

"Really, Snoop!" Brett said, shaking his head.

Snoop didn't budge. He was already dreaming of the day when free range chicken would be on his menu.

Chapter 29
When One Door Closes…

Just as Brett headed out the door for work, Jill hollered up the stairs that it was time for the girls to get ready for school. Coming down the stairs, they immediately went to check on Snoop. Finding him curled up in a ball on the couch, the girls scratched his ears and back, which he always liked.

"Are you okay now, Snoop?" they both asked the dog.

"Your father says he's already been out this morning. He's fine," Jill said.

"Wow!" said Ava. "The only other person I know that could duplicate that feat and survive is Papaw!"

"Yeah," said Brooklyn. "Remember last Christmas when Papaw ate fourteen snickerdoodles in a row before dinner?"

"And he followed that up with two pieces of pumpkin pie right after we ate!" Ava exclaimed.

Jill laughed. Her daughters had a point.

"Your father also said it looked like Snoop was thinking about chasing the chickens this morning!" Jill said.

"Whoa! All that sugar must have given him a burst of energy!" Brooklyn said.

"I hate to burst your bubble," Ava said to Snoop, while scratching his ears, "but there isn't enough sugar in the world to give you the energy you would need to catch one of those chickens! Sorry, Snoop," Ava said, giving him a hug.

"Well, at any rate," Jill said, "anything coming out of the oven that has to cool off from now on is going on top of the refrigerator. As she stared down the dog she said, "Let's see him get up there!"

The Dragonpillar

The school day went by pretty quickly for Ava and Brooklyn. It had been a little over a week since the researchers from Purdue University had been down, and to date, the girls hadn't heard anything back from them. Ava was worried that Mr. Holland might have been told about the 'Dragonpillars', but when homeroom period rolled around, he didn't mention it.

As this was the last day to turn in a specimen, Ava felt somewhat defeated. She had stared at her name on the blackboard every day for the last six weeks, thinking that the blank space beside her name would eventually be filled in, but it hadn't. At least she was not the only one. There were several other students who hadn't turned in anything either.

Toward the end of science class, it seemed to Ava that Mr. Holland made a big deal out of erasing all the names off the blackboard. To Ava, this was almost like pouring salt in her wound. She had tried so hard to find something, but in the back of her mind she knew she had given it her best effort. Even though she hadn't turned a specimen in, she knew that she did indeed have something very special to show for her efforts, although at the moment, she was still trying to keep it a secret.

Right before the period was over, Mr. Holland announced that starting tomorrow, they would begin putting the project together. He told the class what information each student had to provide for their entry and, besides using their laptops to find information, if anyone had any other research materials, they should bring them in as well.

Waiting for the period to end, Ava remembered what Papaw had said to them from time to time: "When one door closes, another door opens". She hoped he was right and hoped she wouldn't have to wait too long for that 'other door' to open.

The next morning, before breakfast, Ava went out on the back 'deck-porch' to check on her tennis shoes. They were completely dry, so she decided to wear them to school. She checked on Mr. Holland's shoes, and they were dry as well. Going back upstairs, she put Mr. Holland's shoes in the same box her tennis shoes had been shipped in.

With her new tennis shoes on, Ava skipped down the stairs into the kitchen to eat breakfast. Brooklyn, already sitting at the table, noticed the shoes immediately as Ava walked in. Brooklyn was about to say something, when Ava held a finger over her lips. Brooklyn nodded, then both girls started to giggle.

"What's so funny this morning?" Jill asked.

"Oh, nothing," they both answered, smiling from ear to ear.

Jill didn't ask any more questions. She just thought to herself, *Wonder what they're up to now?*

At school that day, for science class, Ava decided to leave her laptop in her locker. Although she was going to help her classmates with their entries, she didn't want to accidentally bring up any of the pictures from the meadow she had previously downloaded onto her computer.

However, she did take their large picture book about insects of North America. She wasn't sure if it would help, as there is now a vast amount of material on the internet, but she took it anyway.

The book turned out to be a valuable resource as it contained pictures of the many variations that some insects have, thus making positive identifications much simpler.

Unnoticed by Ava, Mr. Holland seemed to appreciate the fact that Ava was helping her classmates, even though she didn't have an entry in the project.

At the moment, Ava really didn't think about any doors 'closing' or any doors 'opening'. She was simply doing what she liked, helping her classmates with their entries. But for her, one door had definitely just closed but another was about to open.

Later that afternoon when Brett got home from work, as he went through the living room, Ava and Brooklyn were sitting on the couch, watching television. Halfway across the room he stopped, then backed up.

With a look of suspicion, he pointed at Ava's feet. "Where did you get those shoes?"

"What, these shoes?" Ava asked, playfully wiggling her feet.

"Yeah, those shoes. Did Mamaw send you another pair of tennis shoes?" he asked in a rather accusing tone.

"No," answered Ava, enjoying the moment. "These are the shoes I got for my birthday."

Brooklyn was doing her best to keep quiet, enjoying the moment as well.

Brett thought about it for a moment, then hollered, "Jill, come in here a minute!"

Jill came into the room. "What?"

Brett pointed to Ava's shoes.

"Where did you get those shoes?" Jill exclaimed.

Before Ava could answer, Brett asked Jill, "So you don't know anything about this?"

"No, honest, I don't know where she got them," Jill said defensively.

Something's just not adding up here, Brett thought to himself.

"All right, where did you get the shoes?" he asked Ava flatly.

"Out of the creek," Ava said, still smiling.

"Ava Aliese!" Brett said sternly. "Don' tell me any fibs!"

"I'm not!" Ava exclaimed. "Honest!"

Both parents now turned on Brooklyn, figuring she would spill the beans.

Brooklyn simply said, "She's not lying. Me and Ellee were there when she got them out."

"So you got those out of the creek?" Brett asked, still not sure what to believe.

"Yep", Ava said, still smiling.

"How?" her father asked.

Thinking about what to say next, Ava replied, "You wouldn't believe me if I told you." Brooklyn was vigorously nodding her head in agreement.

"I can prove these are the shoes I lost though. Want to bet?" Ava added confidently.

Now Brett and Jill didn't know what to think.

"What's the bet?" Brett asked suspiciously.

"Well, if I'm right, and I know I am," Ava said, "you have to buy me a pony, a real, live pony! If I'm wrong, I'll wash both cars and vacuum them out once a week, until cold weather gets here... and cut the grass around the house once a week, too!" she added.

Now Ava's father was known to be a pretty good poker player and could usually tell when someone was bluffing. He didn't exactly know how, but he knew Ava wasn't bluffing.

"No bet," her father said.

"Darn!" Brooklyn shouted. Pinching her fingers close together she exclaimed, "We were this close to getting a pony!"

"All right," Jill said, "we believe you, but really, how did you get them back?"

"Like I said, you really wouldn't believe most of it, but I will prove these are my shoes."

Ava went upstairs, returning with a shoebox. Handing it to her father she said, "Open it."

Brett opened the box and pulled out the pair of expensive Italian loafers. He had a puzzled look on his face.

"Mr. Holland's shoes," Ava said proudly.

"Good thing I didn't bet," Brett mumbled to Jill. "Brooklyn would have been demanding a pony of her own!"

"Got these out the same time I got my tennis shoes out," Ava said. "Brought both pairs home and cleaned them off with the garden hose. Threw mine in the washer with some towels, then set them out on the back 'deck-porch' to dry," Ava explained. "They turned out pretty good, don't you think?"

Brett looked at Jill. Jill looked at Brett. Brett walked away, shaking his head while heading for the shower. "Don't tell me. I really don't want to know," he said to the girls. "No," he said, holding up his hand, "don't tell me, just don't tell me!"

Looking at the girls, Jill said, "Come on, let's get washed up. It's almost time for supper."

As the girls headed off to the other bathroom, Jill looked at Snoop, who had been sitting on the couch listening the whole time. "You probably had something to do with this, too, didn't you?"

Snoop rolled over on his back, ignoring the accusation. Apparently, Snoop wasn't going to spill the beans either.

Overhearing the conversation from the bathroom, Ava yelled, "Snoop's innocent, mommy. He wasn't there! He stayed home that day to eat your brownies, remember?"

"Oh yeah, that's right! How could I forget?" Jill said, now looking back at the dog with renewed anger. She informed him, "You're still on probation, mister!"

Snoop didn't budge. He was either already asleep or was faking it. In either case, he gave no reaction to the news that his 'probation' had apparently been extended indefinitely.

Chapter 30
The Cave

On Wednesday evening of that week, Mr. Martin from the university called the house to see if it would be all right for them to drive back down this coming Saturday to do more research. Brett told them that would be fine, but Ava and Brooklyn would not be there. Ava had softball practice and Uncle Bryan was taking Brooklyn, Ellee, and Isabelle to a movie that afternoon.

Before Ava left for practice, she told Brooklyn, "They're gonna get a big surprise," as she thought of the strange construction project that had allowed the pond to dry up.

"Yeah, you think they will see it?" Brooklyn asked.

"They can't miss it!" Ava said.

As before, around one p.m. on Saturday, the research team showed up at the farmhouse in the same vehicle. This time, however, the reporter from the local paper, Mr. Koontz, was not with them and conservation officer Barry did not return.

Mr. Martin and his assistants met briefly with Jill, then headed over to the meadow. After nearly three hours, they returned to the farmhouse. Before leaving they again thanked Jill for her hospitality and briefly chatted with her about what they had found.

As they were getting into their car, Brett pulled up with Ava, softball practice apparently over. Before the men could get out of the car, Bryan pulled up as well with the other three girls. Isabelle was still clutching a large bag of half-eaten movie popcorn.

Everyone got out of their vehicles, and Mr. Martin shook the girls' hands once again, saying, "I'm glad you're back. We really wanted to talk to you girls about some very interesting and unusual things we found today."

The girls all traded looks, thinking the men had seen the 'construction project' and the dried-up pond, but they remained silent. Finally Ava asked, "What kind of things?"

"Well," Mr. Martin said, "we followed the creek up to the north, as before, and eventually found the spot where we sat the last time."

The Dragonpillar

Ellee started to say something, but Ava ever so slightly shook her head no.

Mr. Martin continued. "We sat there for quite some time, but none of those insects showed up. We then decided to follow the creek up into the hillside, to see if we could find out where the creek originates."

To Brett he said, "I hope it's all right . We didn't want to climb the barbed-wire fence on that side of your property, so we cut a few of the strands along one fencepost and rolled them back."

"No problem," answered Brett. "We were going to take all of that fence down anyway. We just haven't had time yet."

Mr. Martin looked somewhat relieved. "Yes," he said, "we saw that some of the fence had already been taken down, so we thought it would be all right."

At this point, Ava was thinking to herself that it was odd that no one had yet made any mention of the pond being dried up, or the strange looking construction project that had diverted the water. Looking at Brooklyn and Ellee, Ava could tell they were thinking the same thing.

"From here," Mr. Martin continued, "we followed the creek up into the woods, onto the hillside. Eventually, it led us to a rocky outcropping concealing the entrance to a small cave. We discovered that the creek is flowing from somewhere out of the back of this cave. However, we were not able to go in as the opening is very small, too small for a person to fit through."

"A cave?" asked Ellee.

"Yes, a cave," replied Mr. Martin.

"Using our flashlights," one of Mr. Martin's assistants said, "we were able to see back several feet into the cave, but then the walls make a sharp turn, and that's as far back as we could see in."

Mr. Martin then asked, "Have any of you girls ever been up there to this spot?"

All the girls shook their heads no.

"What about any of you parents?" he asked, looking around at all the adults.

They all shook their heads as well. "We didn't know there was a cave up there," said Brett.

Mr. Martin looked as if he didn't get the answer he was expecting. Rubbing his chin, he said, "As we followed the creek north, we recorded water temperatures at regular intervals along the way. We found that the creek is indeed being fed by a warm spring, probably back in that cave, and the water temperatures increased the closer we got to it. This means, more than likely, that in this area, the creek probably never freezes over in the winter. It's also quite possible that the plant life close to the water and near the cave opening might survive through the winter months as well, due to the supply of warm water keeping the plants from freezing."

With this new information, Ellee was beginning to come up with a startling theory of her own. She leaned over and whispered to Ava. Ava's mouth dropped open in shock and surprise.

Her reaction didn't go unnoticed by Mr. Martin. He said, "A couple of my assistants think it's quite possible that these insects use this cave, possibly as a nest or hive of sorts. If that is the case, it's also quite possible that they themselves might actually be able to survive through the winter months as well, much as hornets do that hibernate in the large, round, paper-like hives they build or maybe by living in a semi-dormant stage all winter long. In either case, if their food source doesn't die off due to the cold weather, it's quite possible that they could survive through the winter months."

Ellee was nodding her head in agreement, having already theorized this for herself. But she was thinking though, that it might be even more extraordinary than the researchers yet realized.

"Why do you think these insects use that cave?" asked Bryan. "Have you seen some going in, or coming out?"

"Well, no, not exactly," said Mr. Martin, "but something is using that cave. And those peculiar flowers are all over the place up there... and there's something else."

"Something else?" asked Brett.

Before Mr. Martin went any further, he asked the girls again, "Are you sure none of you have ever been up there before?"

"No, never. Why?" they all answered.

Getting a little irritated at the girls being grilled with the same question they had already answered, Brett said, "Okay, what's this all about?"

The Dragonpillar

"I'm sorry," apologized Mr. Martin. "I just had to be sure and you will understand why," he added. Hesitating, and choosing his words carefully, he finally said, "Well, this is where it gets really weird."

"What do you mean weird?" asked Brooklyn.

"Well... we're still scratching our heads on this one," he said. "All over the ground up there, near the entrance to that cave, are literally hundreds, if not thousands, of neat little piles of small sticks and twigs."

"It's the woods!" said Brett. "What's so weird about sticks and twigs on the ground in the woods?"

"Well," Mr. Martin said slowly, "for some reason, these sticks and twigs appear to have been sorted by size and length, then neatly stacked. There are so many of these stacks we didn't have time to count them all. Each stack consists of sticks and twigs, all about the same length and diameter, and the stacks are even lined up in rows! To me, the whole thing resembles a miniature construction site, where contractors have building materials stockpiled on the property, prior to actual construction. It's really strange! We've never, and I mean never have we seen anything like this before!"

Mr. Martin let everyone digest that information, then showed them some of the pictures they had taken of this strange phenomena.

Looking at the pictures, Brett and Bryan looked a little dubious, now wondering if the girls had indeed been up there and had done this, but for who knows what reason. But seeing that the girls were as much in the dark about this as everyone else, they quickly dismissed the idea.

"If these insects are really doing this," Mr. Martin said, pointing to the camera, "it would almost certainly have to imply that, as strange as it sounds, these insects might have a fairly high level of intelligence. This type of behavior would point to planning and preparation, for some purpose that we cannot fathom at this moment. We have no idea how or why they would behave in such a fashion, but it is certainly extraordinary. Right now, although we can't account for this strange behavior, if this proves to be the case, this will truly be a major discovery in the field of entomology."

Watching the girls' reaction to this revelation, Mr. Martin was now positive the girls had nothing to do with it, but he was also was positive they knew more about this than they were telling.

As Mr. Martin and his assistants were preparing to leave, Ava asked, "Did you see anything else that looked strange?"

Mr. Martin was caught off guard by the question. Now he was sure the girls knew something that they were not sharing, but he decided not to ask any further questions. "No", he said, "that's all we saw, but that in itself is enough for any scientist for one day!"

As they prepared to leave again, Mr. Martin told the parents he would keep in touch. However, with these new discoveries, any conclusions that his team might have come up with regarding the insects would now, more than likely, be pushed back even further as much more study and research would now be needed to prove or disprove what they had discovered today.

As the men drove off, Ava exclaimed, "I knew it, I knew it! I knew it all along!"

"Knew what?" Brett asked.

"That these insects are smart," said Ava.

"How do you know that?" asked Bryan.

"I don't know," Ava said, shrugging her shoulders. "I could just tell, I guess."

Brett and Bryan just rolled their eyes. They suspected as well that the girls knew more about the insects than they were telling, but Brett just said, "After pitching batting practice for two straight hours, all I care about right now is finding something cold to drink and getting some ice on my sore elbow!"

Chapter 31
Rumors

The next couple of weeks went by very quickly for all four girls, as usually is the case this time of year. With not only homework piling up with the end of the school year drawing near, Ava was involved with softball several nights a week.

Two evenings a week, and on Saturday mornings, Ellee and Isabelle were now involved in gymnastics.

Brooklyn was practicing two nights a week for the upcoming fourth grade class play. She had the lead role of 'Queen Elsa' in the play 'Frozen', from the Disney movie. When she landed the part, the teachers found out that the school did not even have to buy or make her costumes, as she already had her own, and of course, she already knew the words to every song.

It was now the second week of May. The rumor going around the school was that Mr. Holland was moving at the end of the school year, having taken a teaching position in another city.

The third and fourth graders became obsessed with finding out if the rumor was true, but none of them could find anything out, or even where the rumor had started. Ava and Brooklyn suspected that since their mother was a teacher at the school, surely if the rumor was true, she would know something.

One evening, around the supper table, Brooklyn asked, "Mommy, have you heard anything about Mr. Holland moving after this school year is over?"

"No, Brooklyn, I haven't heard anything about that, just the same rumors you've heard going around the school. Why do you ask?" Jill said.

"Oh, just wondering," Brooklyn said.

"All the kids at school are talking about it," Ava said.

"I'm sure if it were true, I would have already heard about it," Jill said, dashing Brooklyn's hopes. "You know how rumors get started," she added.

The girls went back to finishing their supper. "Darn it!" exclaimed Brooklyn under her breath.

As Ava no longer needed to look for a specimen for her class project, no one had been over to the meadow for nearly two weeks, not since Ava had recovered her shoes. This Friday, however, Ellee and Isabelle were staying over for the weekend, as their parents were attending a class reunion and would be out of town. Ava and Brooklyn had already talked to their father about it, and he said if the weather was nice, he might give everyone a ride around the farm on Saturday.

Sure enough, mid-morning on Saturday, Brett pulled the Gator out of the barn and hooked up the trailer. The girls all piled on, with Snoop again being hoisted up by his frustrated owner. This time no butterfly nets or collection jars were taken along. However, Isabelle was still packing the binoculars, just in case. Snoop took his usual spot on the trailer, front and center, as the girls fussed over him. Brett just looked at the dog and shook his head, making the girls giggle. It seemed they knew something their father didn't.

Brett gave them a really long ride around the farm and eventually wound up driving through the meadow. The going was a little more difficult as the vegetation had grown even higher and thicker in the last couple of weeks. However, this presented no real problem for the four-wheel drive utility vehicle. Curious to see if the insects were still around, Brett drove up to the area where the girls had found the log, and shut the engine off. The girls, up to this point, were noisily chatting, but now decided to quiet down. The silence only lasted a few seconds.

Brooklyn shouted, "Ava, look!" pointing in the direction of the pond. Brett turned, thinking she had seen one of the insects, but didn't see anything out of the ordinary. The girls, on the other hand, did.

Staring at the pond, Ava exclaimed, "What happened?"

"Rains must have washed it away," Ellee whispered.

The pond had filled back up with water and there was no sign of the small dike or the wall that had diverted the water around it.

"What washed away?" Brett questioned the girls, having heard what Ellee had whispered.

"Err… nothing, Uncle Brett," Ellee said. "We thought maybe some beavers were building a hut over there," she said, pointing out over the water, "but it's not there anymore. I guess it wasn't what we thought it was."

"Oh, okay," Brett said, accepting the hastily thought of explanation.

On the ride back to the farmhouse, the girls talked in hushed tones. "What do you think really happened to it?" asked Brooklyn.

"I don't know," said Ellee, "but I don't think we've had enough rain lately to wash it away."

After thinking about that for a moment, Ava spoke up. "That's probably why the researchers never mentioned it, because it wasn't there."

"Well, if it didn't wash away," Brooklyn said, "what happened to it?"

"I'd say whoever built it, must have torn it down," said Ava. The girls just looked at each other in amazement, realizing the implications of what Ava had just proposed.

"Well, at any rate," Brooklyn added, "whatever might have happened, that's one rumor you won't be hearing at school anytime soon."

Chapter 32
The Sky is Falling

That afternoon, before leaving town to attend his class reunion, Bryan and Lee Ann stopped by Ava's to make sure Ellee and Isabelle had everything they needed for the weekend. "You girls going to mind Uncle Brett and Aunt Jill?" they asked.

"Don't worry," Jill said, "they're never any trouble. The only one I have trouble with is him!" Jill said, pointing to Snoop.

Snoop just stared at Jill with a smug look on his face, apparently thinking the 'brownie incident' was going to be brought up again. Lee Ann laughed, having heard from Bryan about the disappearing brownies.

That night, the girls were upstairs sitting around in their pajamas. It was too early for bed, so they were talking about school and all the rumors going around about Mr. Holland.

Snoop was already hauled up on Ava's bed, his feet sticking up in the air, snoring as usual. Ava attempted to shove Snoop to one side of the bed in order to get enough of the sheets pulled up to sleep under.

"Move over and be quiet!" she chastised the dog. She was only able to scoot him over a few inches before giving up. "It's like having a four-legged, hairy block of concrete lying across your ankles!" Ava said in frustration.

"Actually," Ellee said, "I think a block of concrete weighs less." The girls all laughed.

For spite, Ava showed the other girls how to tickle the hairs inside Snoop's ears and the hairs between the pads of his feet. When she did that, his ears and feet would twitch. They all took turns, laughing all the while they were tormenting the dog. However, Snoop didn't even wake up.

"How can he sleep so much?" asked Isabelle.

"Beats me," said Ava. "Every day we get home from school he is on the couch either sleeping or watching television."

"Your dog watches television?" Ellee asked incredulously.

"Well, I don't know if he is actually watching it or not, but it's on and he's looking at the screen," said Brooklyn.

Isabelle asked excitedly, "What do you think his favorite TV show is?"

The giggling started again. They all took turns trying to guess what Snoop's favorite show would be.

Finally, Ava said, "He probably watches just to see the dog food commercials!"

"Good call!" said Ellee, laughing uncontrollably. They all agreed that Ava had nailed it.

After the girls became bored with teasing the dog, Brooklyn, in a serious tone asked, "Ava, do you think there really was a bull up there around the shed when I found that rope?"

Ava thought about it for a moment before deciding what to say. "Well, it doesn't really matter," she said, "whether it was up there or not. You thought it was, so what you did was still a really brave thing."

Ava could tell that her sister seemed really glad to hear that.

"Yeah," Brooklyn answered, "but do you think it was really up there?" she asked again.

"Remember," Ava said, "when I got called downstairs to find out about my punishment?" Brooklyn nodded.

"Well, I asked Daddy about that very thing. He said the bull was up there when we bought the farm, but before we moved in, Mr. Gray and a bunch of men corralled it, pushed it into the back of his truck, and delivered it to another farm," Ava said. "That's why we've never seen it. It was gone by the time we moved in. But up until Daddy told me that, I believed what he originally told us, and I thought myself that it was up there somewhere in the meadow or the woods."

"That's what I was thinking, too," said Brooklyn. "But why did Daddy tell us that in the first place?"

"Daddy told us that because he said that part of the meadow is pretty far from the house and he didn't want us trying to climb that barbed-wire fence," Ava said. "The story about those four senior boys a few years ago getting beaten up by that bull and then getting cut up on that fence is true.

"Also, Daddy said that Papaw's brother, when he was about our age, slipped while climbing a barbed-wire fence just like that one. It cut up his hands and face pretty badly, but Daddy said it could have been much worse. So Daddy knew how dangerous that fence could be."

"So Daddy lied to us?" Brooklyn asked.

"Well, sort of," replied Ava.

Before Ava could explain any further, Isabelle excitedly asked, "So did Uncle Brett's nose grow any longer?" as she now was taking a real interest in what Ava was saying.

"What are you talking about?"Ellee asked.

"You know," said Isabelle, "like Pinolkeeoh! Whenever he tells a lie, his nose grows longer!"

The other three girls tried not to laugh.

"I think you mean Pinocchio," said Ellee.

"Yeah, that's what I said, Pinolkeeoh," countered Isabelle.

"No, his nose didn't grow any longer," said Ava.

"Oh," said Isabelle, now looking clearly disappointed.

Continuing where she left off Ava said, "Daddy explained it this way. He said this is what adults call a 'white lie'."

"White lie?" they all questioned. "What's that?"

"It's rather difficult to explain, but I'll try," said Ava.

"Daddy said, for instance, if he knows that you want to do something that is bad for you or something that might get you injured, like climbing that barbed-wire fence, then he might make up a scary story about what it is you are wanting to do, to frighten you into not doing it. Hopefully, by scaring you, he will have saved you from getting injured or getting into trouble." Ava let that sink in for a while.

"Like I said, it's sort of difficult to explain," Ava added. "Daddy thought that by just telling us not to climb that barbed-wire fence, we wouldn't see the danger in it, and might go ahead and try to climb it anyway. So he told us the 'white lie', about the bull still being up there, to scare us to the point where we wouldn't try and go over that fence no matter what. He didn't exactly tell us the truth, but he didn't exactly tell us a lie either. That's what a 'white lie' is."

The other three girls were silent, and Ava could tell they were each processing the information in their own way.

Ava decided to try another approach. "Let me give you another example. Brooklyn, do you remember when we first moved in here and Daddy told you to stay out of the loft in the barn?"

"Yeah," Brooklyn said cautiously.

"Well, he just didn't want you climbing that old rickety, wooden ladder. He thought it would either break or you would simply fall off. He also didn't want you to get near those upper windows in the barn because they are always open and you might accidentally fall out one of them, and that's a long way to the ground! So he just told you the 'boogeyman' lived up there. You were so scared, we couldn't even get you to go into the barn at all after that, even when we had your birthday party in there!" Ava said, laughing.

"Yeah, I can't believe I fell for that line," Brooklyn said, shaking her head. "Everyone knows there is no such thing as the 'boogeyman.'"

"Well, see? That was a 'white lie'," Ava said.

Isabelle, who up until now had still not received a satisfactory answer about Pinocchio, piped up again. "What's this about no boogeyman?" she exclaimed, frowning suspiciously at her sister.

Ellee was now glaring at Brooklyn, giving her the '*thanks a lot*' look.

Oops! thought Ava. *Apparently the 'boogeyman' is still being used as an enforcement tool at their house! But now, probably not much longer, if at all. Isabelle is a quick learner.*

At this point, it was getting late and the conversation was beginning to die down. Ava again attempted to move Snoop over so she could get under the covers.

"Darn it, Snoop!" Ava said, scolding the dog, as if he had a choice about instantly reducing his weight.

Leaning down from the top bunk, Brooklyn said, "Ava, you can put him up here with me tonight, if you want."

Ava got out of bed, and with Brooklyn's assistance, they attempted to hoist the semi-unconscious Snoop to the top bunk. Isabelle watched in horror.

"It's not going to work," Ava said. "He's too heavy. We can't lift him up that high and he certainly won't climb up the ladder. Maybe when Mommy and Daddy come in to check on us later, I'll have Daddy put him up there with you."

This answer seemed to satisfy Brooklyn for the moment, and she lay back down and crawled under her sheets.

Ellee, just out of curiosity, asked, "Ava, he ever fall out of bed?"

"Mmm… not that I know of, why?"

"Just wondering," Ellee whispered. Then she added, "Hope you're right. Somebody down here might get squashed!"

The girls eventually drifted off to sleep, except for Isabelle. She was remembering the story her teacher had read the class that morning about Chicken Little, who ran around yelling, "The sky is falling, the sky is falling!"

She now thought she knew what Chicken Little was talking about." She pulled the covers up over her head, curled up in a tight ball, and prayed Chicken Little was wrong.

Chapter 33
An Urban Legend is Born

During the next week, the girls had pretty much finished up work on their 4-H exhibit. Mr. Nelson came by once again to check on their progress. He was impressed with what they had done, and told them so.

"This is going to be a very popular exhibit this year," he said. "You girls have done an excellent job. I can't wait to see it displayed and see the public's reaction. I think everyone will really enjoy this!"

His comments made the girls feel proud of their efforts and the fact that all the work each had put into the project was already being appreciated.

When Mamaw and Papaw came by that week, Ava and Brooklyn showed them the nearly completed exhibit.

Papaw liked it so much, that after reading the information Ava had written up, he said, "You know, Ava, one day this might make for an interesting book. When you have time, what you should do is write down everything you can remember about this adventure and as other events unfold, write them down as well. Save all your notes in a folder and one of these days, you never know, you might want to write a book about the 'Dragonpillars.'"

"I like that idea, Papaw," Ava said, now thinking along those lines.

"I think that's a good idea, too," said Jill.

Ava nodded. Maybe the seed had been planted, maybe not. However, it would probably be years, though, before anyone would ever find out if that seed would indeed bear fruit.

At the end of the week, on Saturday, Ava had one of her last remaining league games at Lassie League Field. Her league team was made up of girls from both the fourth and fifth grades.

The third base line of the diamond they were playing on that evening ran parallel to Emerson Drive, a main artery that led into a nearby subdivision. However, for safety reasons, the playing field was separated from the street by a sidewalk and an eight foot high chain link fence. Occasionally foul balls would go over the fence, and one of the parents sitting in the bleachers along that baseline would go and retrieve them.

That night, before the game started, the rumor again circulating around the park was that Mr. Holland was moving right after school was over. However, none of the players still had any information that this was indeed the case. Among the girls, though, it still made for good gossip.

To make matters even more interesting, Mr. Holland lived in the neighborhood close to the park, and as the game got underway, one of the players saw him drive right past their diamond on Emerson. Most of the girls knew what type of truck he drove due to the boys in Ava's class, who had already staked out his house and truck for this year's Halloween 'payback'.

Suddenly, one of the players sitting on the third base bench yelled, "Here he comes again!"

The players on both benches rushed to the fence, as well as all the players on the field from both teams, just in time to see Mr. Holland drive by again, this time with a truckload of furniture and a U-Haul trailer hitched to the back.

All the parents in attendance that evening can attest to the fact that the spontaneous cheer that erupted from the fourth grade students, to this day, has never been equaled in volume or intensity, and more than likely never will be.

Gloves and hats were thrown into the air, and the high-fiving among the players went on for several minutes. The poor umpire tried to restore order. He kept yelling, "Play ball! Play ball!"

But the players paid no attention. The parents sitting in the bleachers on both sides were just as confused as the umpire.

As soon as Mr. Holland's truck disappeared from view, Ava was picked up by members from both teams and carried on shoulders around the bases for a victory lap. Parents later reported that a chorus of, "Ding dong the wicked witch is dead," could be heard being sung by the players as they marched around the bases.

One of the parents sitting in the bleachers said, "I've heard them sing 'God Bless America' after a few innings, but I don't get this!"

The Dragonpillar

Several parents sitting on the bleachers with Ava's parents were looking at them for answers, but Jill just shrugged her shoulders, feigning ignorance.

Just as the frustrated umpire was able to get order restored and the game restarted, as the student calling the game from the press box was about to announce the next batter's name, through an open mike everyone heard the scorekeeper sitting next to him say, "I guess we don't have to worry about that creep anymore!" Then they could be heard snickering. This ignited another round of cheering and uncontrollable laughter from both benches.

When the game was finally over and the parents were filing off the bleachers, Brett whispered to Jill, "What was that all about?"

"The kids saw Mr. Holland drive by with a truckload of his furniture," Jill replied.

"Oh... Oh!" exclaimed Brett, now realizing what had caused all the commotion. "No wonder!"

Over time, in their town that game became an urban legend, and even to this day, no one can remember the score of the game, or even if an actual winner was decided. The fourth grade players, though, from both teams, at that time all said it was the best 'early' Christmas present they had ever received.

Chapter 34
Welcome to the 21ˢᵗ Century

The following week being the last week of school, the students only had to go a half-day on Friday. As homeroom had been Ava's last class each day, she therefore had no homeroom period that day. She was finally finished with Mr. Holland, or so she thought.

At noon on Friday, report cards were handed out and parents had previously been notified that they had to sign their student's report card and mail or take it back in to the school office. In doing so, this ensured that the child's parent or guardian would actually *see* the report card, instead of possibly having the report card thrown in a trash can on the student's way out of school, as had happened in some cases as reported by the school janitors cleaning out the trash cans that evening.

Ava didn't bother to open the envelope her report card was in. She already knew the grade she was getting in each subject, so she just stuck the envelope in her backpack and forgot about it.

Riding home from school, the girls could tell that Jill was in a very good mood. Other than finishing up some paperwork and cleaning out her classroom on Monday, she was now off for summer break with the rest of the students. The girls figured that was the reason for the good mood she was in.

The girls themselves were in a very good mood as well. Even though they all liked school, they were all looking forward to all the fun things they would get to do over summer break.

"Guess what?" Jill asked, looking in the rearview mirror. "I have a surprise!"

"We love surprises!" the girls all said excitedly.

Brooklyn went first, trying to guess what the surprise was. "Mmm… we're putting in a pool?"

Jill laughed. "Well, not that big of a surprise."

The Dragonpillar

"Daddy bought us a pony?" Ava said excitedly.

"Uh... no, no pony," Jill answered. "Sorry." Jill hadn't expected that one.

Ellee and Isabelle made no attempts at guessing what the surprise might be. They figured it was probably just for Ava and Brooklyn anyway, although a swimming pool would have been sweet.

"I'll just tell you," Jill said. "We're all going out for pizza tonight at your favorite restaurant!"

"Yes! No leftovers tonight!" Ava exclaimed, laughing.

Now, normally that outburst would immediately be followed by a sermon on the virtues of not wasting food. However, in this instance, Jill let it slide.

"Aunt Jill, are we going, too?" asked Ellee cautiously.

"Yep, we're all going," she replied. "As soon as everyone gets home from work and cleaned up, we're going to meet you guys there."

"Awesome!" said Ellee, giving Ava and Brooklyn the customary 'knuckles'.

"Other than school being out," Ava asked, "any other occasion for celebration?" She was thinking that maybe Mr. Gordon or Mr. Martin had called, so she asked, "Did the people from the university call?"

Trying not to give anything away by smiling too much, Jill said, "No they didn't call. We haven't heard a word from them."

Jill was telling the girls the truth, although there was much more she wasn't telling them.

"Oh, okay," Ava replied, somewhat disappointed. "That sure is taking a long time," she added.

"Yes," Jill said. "Remember the last time they were here? They said it was probably going to take longer than they originally thought because of their new findings. I'm sure, though, that we we'll find out something soon," Jill said, trying to hide a chuckle.

"Maybe we should call them," Ellee offered.

"That's a good idea. We'll call them first thing Monday morning to see if they know anything yet. Okay with you, Ava?" Jill added.

"Yeah, I guess so," Ava said.

Early that evening, after Brett, Bryan, and Lee Ann had gotten home from work and had a chance to change clothes, they all piled into their cars and met at the girl's favorite pizza place.

When the two families walked in, the staff had already reserved a large table for the eight of them.

"I didn't know you could make reservations here," Ava said. No one answered.

As they were seated, Ava noticed that her mother had carried in a large plastic shopping bag with something rolled up inside, which she laid on the floor at her feet.

For a moment, Ava thought that maybe it was a gift and this was a surprise birthday get-together for someone in the family. She mentally ran down all the birthdates she knew, and quickly realized that no one in their group was celebrating a birthday that night or anytime soon.

As they placed their order, it seemed to Ava that the waitress was being overly friendly and Ava also noticed the workers, back in the kitchen area, whispering and pointing in their direction. The other three girls noticed it too. They began whispering back and forth between themselves, trying to figure out what was going on.

As the pizza was brought out, the girls noticed other patrons in the dining area gawking and pointing in their direction as well. They were now sure something was up, but hunger overtook their curiosity, and they tore into the pizza, forgetting about everything else.

As the last few slices of pizza were consumed, the parents sat back in their chairs, enjoying the moment. Ava looked up and noticed all four parents were watching them instead of talking amongst themselves, as was usually the case. Ava whispered something to the other three girls, and they all looked up. The table got quiet and Ava sensed someone was about to make a speech.

Ellee must have gotten straight 'As' again, Ava thought to herself.

Brett cleared his throat. The girls knew this was the signal to 'listen up'. "We are proud of all the hard work each of you has put in this year at school," he began.

Looking at Brooklyn and Ellee, Ava thought again, *Yep, someone got straight 'As.'*

The Dragonpillar

"And," Bryan added," we are especially proud of the way you all handled your punishment by agreeing to do the fair exhibit, and all the hard work you have done on it."

"Hopefully," Brett now said, as Jill handed him the plastic bag she had brought in, "you can still add this to your exhibit."

Brett pulled the evening's paper out of the bag. Taking off the rubber band and unrolling it, he laid it down in front of the girls. On the front was a half-page color picture of one of the pictures Mr. Koontz had taken over in the meadow that day of the girls sitting on the log with Snoop at their feet.

The headline read: Local girls find new species of insect on farm. Girls name insects 'Dragonpillars'. Flowers found turn out to be new species as well. Flowers named 'Pink Bobbys'. Story by A. Koontz.

Below the picture was a half-page article Mr. Koontz had written about their discovery from all the information he had collected that day.

The girls were speechless. As they tried to read the article, the pizza parlor erupted into applause.

Finally recovering from the shock and surprise, Ava said to her mother, "You already knew this before we came here, didn't you?"

"Mmm… maybe," Jill said, smiling.

The girls got out of their seats and gave their parents hugs. The room erupted into applause again.

"This beats getting an 'A' in science class any day!" Ava said.

At this point, the waitress brought out a bowl of ice cream covered with chocolate syrup and sprinkles for each girl.

"On the house!" she said.

Even before starting on her ice cream, Ellee produced a small tape measure from her backpack, of course, and was already figuring out what size frame they would need to properly mount the newspaper picture and article for their 4-H exhibit.

When Ava and Brooklyn got home that night, they excitedly showed the picture in the newspaper to Snoop.

"Look, Snoop! You're a celebrity!" they said. Snoop sniffed the paper, quickly deducing it wasn't edible. He looked questioningly back up at both girls.

157

"I bet he's trying to figure out a way to parlay his newfound celebrity status into a larger share of doggie treats," Jill said. They all laughed.

Sensing all the excitement and hearing all the laughter, Snoop knew this was a good sign. Hopefully, the discussion of his weight problem and impending diet would at least be put off for another day.

Chapter 35
The Only Constant in Life is Change

Then next afternoon, on Sunday, Jill was sitting at the kitchen table, finishing up some paperwork for school. "Ava, Brooklyn, bring me your report cards," Jill yelled. "I have to sign and turn them in tomorrow."

Brooklyn, with report card in hand, was the first to show up in the kitchen. "Why tomorrow?"

"I have to turn this paperwork in tomorrow and clean out my classroom, so I might as well turn your report cards in at the same." Continuing, she said, "You girls will have to go with me because Daddy will be at work."

Jill opened Brooklyn's report card, quickly scanning down the list of subjects. "Nice job, Brooky!" she said. "Your teacher says there are some areas you need to improve on, but overall, that's a good report," She gave Brooklyn a hug.

Ava filed into the kitchen, handing her the unopened envelope her grade card was in. Taking the envelope, Jill asked, "How did you do this grading period?"

"Okay, I guess," replied Ava. Jill could tell the envelope hadn't been opened. Opening the envelope, Jill scanned down the list of subjects.

"Nice job, Ava. Jill scanned down the list: 'A's and 'B's' and one 'C'.

"Well, your teachers say there are a couple of areas you need to work on as well, but..." Jill stopped. She paused, momentarily, staring at the card. Ava immediately thought something was wrong.

"Congratulations!" Jill exclaimed. "Why didn't you tell us?"

"Tell you what?" Ava asked, totally lost.

Jill just handed her the report card so she could see for herself.

From top to bottom, her classes were listed in the same order she had had them each school day. So the very last one at the bottom of the card was homeroom period.

The report card read: *Homeroom – Science 'A'*, not 'A-minus' as Ava was expecting!

Ava stammered, "I... I don't get it. I didn't turn anything in. Mr. Holland must have made a mistake."

"Did you do some extra credit or something?" Jill asked.

"Mr. Holland doesn't give extra credit," Ava said.

Ava thought about it for a moment, then said, "Maybe you can call him and find out."

"Well," Jill said, "I don't want to bother him at home on a Sunday, so why don't we wait until tomorrow. We'll probably be able to catch him at school, and then we can ask him, all right?"

"All right," Ava replied, still staring at the report card, trying to figure out what had happened.

After Ava had walked out of the kitchen, Jill called Mr. Holland at his house, but there was no answer. She left a message for him to call her, if he didn't get back in too late.

Later in the day, Jill asked the girls, "You know what today is?" They looked at her with blank stares.

"No, what?" they both asked.

"Two weeks from today, we have to take your 4-H exhibit over to the fair!"

"That's right!" they said. "We almost forgot!"

On Monday, as they went down the hall to Jill's classroom, she stopped by Mr. Holland's room. The door was unlocked, so she went in and turned the lights on. To her surprise, she saw that his classroom had already been cleaned out. She turned off the lights and closed the door.

When they got to her classroom, she left Ava and Brooklyn there and went down to the office. After turning in their report cards, she learned that Mr. Holland was already in the process of moving and did not leave a number where he could immediately be reached.

The school secretary told Jill that Mr. Holland had accepted a teaching position in another city, and wanted to be settled in his new home at least a month before the start of the next school year. That meant he would still be around town at least for a few more weeks, so Jill should still be able to get in touch with him. Jill thanked her for the information, then returned to her classroom.

Telling Ava what she found out, she said, "Don't worry, Ava. I left a message at the office and at his home for him to call me. He'll call back when he gets home."

Chapter 36
The Exhibit Set-Up

Before they knew it, the girls were loading up their exhibit to take to the fair.

"Wow! That two weeks went by quickly!" Ava said, as she was helping the other three girls load up the components of their exhibit into the back of their car.

"Yeah, I can't believe the fair starts next Saturday!" said Brooklyn, as she carefully placed the framed 'Pink Bobbys' into the backseat of their SUV.

Ellee slid the newly-framed newspaper article about their discovery, as well as a book containing most of the pictures she had taken in the meadow, into the backseat as well. The girls had originally wanted to include the pictures Ellee had taken of the men dragging Mr. Holland out of the mud with the rope Brooklyn had found, but as soon as their parents found out, it was strongly suggested that they leave those out.

Isabelle's parents had several of her favorite sketches framed as well. As they helped Isabelle carefully load her artwork in with the rest of the exhibit, it was outwardly apparent that she was proud of the fact that she had made a contribution to the project.

"Those are really good, Izzy!" Ava told her. "You're not only a good artist, you're the best 'lookout' we ever had!"

Isabelle beamed, not knowing that she was the *only* lookout the girls had ever had, or needed, for that matter.

When they arrived at the fairgrounds, they had no trouble finding the exhibit building for agricultural entries. As you walked through the main entrance, all the 4-H exhibit buildings were on your right, just past the conservation department's concrete fish tanks and small display tent.

However, they did not have to carry all their stuff from the parking lot, as they were allowed to drive right up to the entrance of their exhibit building to unload their materials.

The Dragonpillar

The exhibit building was larger than their barn. It had recently been painted with a fresh coat of white paint, and the large, black letters above the sliding doors read: *Exhibit Building No. 4*. These had been recently repainted as well.

As they unloaded their project and walked in, they could see that few exhibits had been set up, as most of the exhibit tables were still bare.

The tables were arranged in long rows along the outside walls, and ran the entire length of the building on both sides. Down the center of the floor was a dividing aisle of almost the same length, with tables set up along both sides of it as well. To the girls, the nearly-empty building looked enormous. Ava couldn't imagine that in a few days, all that table space would be taken up, and then some.

Shortly after they began unloading their materials, Mr. Nelson arrived to show the girls where to set up their exhibit. Everyone followed Mr. Nelson to the mid-way point of the first row of tables, along the outside wall to the right, when he stopped. Apparently, their exhibit was to be on display almost directly in the center of the exhibit building.

"This looks like an awfully good spot for their first time," Brett said to Mr. Nelson.

"Well," Mr. Nelson chuckled," their project looks great and we didn't want anyone to miss it. Sometimes when exhibits are set up in the corners of the buildings, people tell us after the fair that they didn't see them. So we decided to showcase their exhibit."

Examining their finished project, Mr. Nelson said, "Fairgoers are really going to enjoy this, especially since their discovery was on the front page of the paper recently. A lot of people are still talking about it."

As he saw other people entering the exhibit building, Mr. Nelson said, "I need to help some of these people get their projects set up as well, so I need to go. Good luck with your exhibit."

As he walked back to the entrance of the building, Ellee asked, "What did he mean when he said, 'good luck with your exhibit'?"

"I'm not sure," said Ava. "Maybe he just meant that he hopes none of this stuff gets broken during the fair," she said. "If any of those pictures get knocked over, the glass might break!"

"Probably," said Brooklyn, now scooting her framed flowers a little further back from the edge of the table.

Chapter 37
The 4-H Fair

The next Saturday, the fair officially began. All four parents decided to take the girls that weekend, especially since they had been 'bugging' them all week about seeing the exhibits and going on the rides. So on Sunday after church, they all piled into two cars and followed each other to the fairgrounds.

Coming in the main entrance, they had to walk past the exhibit buildings before getting to the midway where the rides are, so they decided to check out the exhibits first, but not before stopping at the concrete fish tanks to toss pennies at the snapping turtles.

Lee Ann said to the girls, "I think you're supposed to make a wish when you do that," referring to the money being 'donated' for turtle conservation. The girls just looked at her, holding out their hands for more coins.

As they walked through the wide, open sliding door of Exhibit Building No. 4, the girls were amazed. The tables were completely crammed with all kinds of projects and exhibits relating to science and agriculture. Somehow, the interior of the building now did not look quite as spacious as it had a week earlier, when it was nearly empty. And of course, there were lots of people milling around, looking at all the various entries, which made it look even smaller.

To view the exhibits, they had to get in line to the right as they came through the wide entrance. The crowd seemed to be flowing mostly down the right side, then around the far end, and then back up toward the front, along the opposite wall.

"No use going against the flow," said Bryan, as they all got in line.

As the line began to slowly move, the crowd seemed to thin out somewhat. The girls could see colored ribbons; red, white, and blue, scattered among the exhibits. Apparently everything had been judged before the fair started, which made sense.

They hadn't gone very far when up ahead, Ava spied a familiar case with a blue ribbon attached. It was her class insect project. Ava felt a wave of mixed emotions come over her. "Oh well," she sighed, as they got closer.

The Dragonpillar

As they came up to the table where her class project sat, all the girls now could see the blue ribbon attached to the case. "My class got a blue ribbon again," Ava said flatly to everyone.

"I thought her class project always got Grand Champion," Jill whispered to Brett. "I wonder what exhibit got that award then this year?"

As the group got close enough to actually look down inside the case at the insects, Ava's heart almost stopped. Mounted in the center of the bottom row, in perfect condition, was the most remarkable yellow butterfly she had ever seen. Yet, somehow… it looked familiar.

"It couldn't be!" she whispered to herself.

Listed below the butterfly was its corresponding entry number, #117.

Ava nearly pushed her father out of the way getting to the master list attached to the other side of the case. She quickly scanned down the row of numbers to #117. To the right of the number it read: Tiger Swallowtail. Entered by Ava R.

Everyone just stared in disbelief, except for Isabelle, who was squawking for someone to pick her up so she could see.

Ava turned to her mother, almost in tears, and said, "Mommy, I didn't turn… " her voice trailed off, still trying to comprehend what was going on.

"You don't suppose…?" Jill asked Brett.

"After the last two months, nothing would surprise me," Brett said, shaking his head in disbelief as well.

They all stood there, staring at the butterfly. The only explanation that made sense to Brett and Jill was that this was the same butterfly Ava had taken to school two years earlier, when she was in the third grade. The same butterfly that Mr. Holland had taken off the desk of Ava's third grade teacher, the day she had show-n-tell.

"I… I just can't believe it," Ava stammered, but somehow she knew.

Putting things into perspective, as she often did, Ellee said, "Apparently Mr. Holland has some redeeming qualities that we were not aware of."

Recovering from the shock somewhat and with the crowd now starting to push them along Jill said, pointing to the tables up ahead, "Let's keep moving. I want to see what all those people are looking at."

As they inched closer, the girls could see a rather large group admiring an exhibit, but because of all the people, it was difficult for them to see exactly what was on the table.

As the girls walked up, the strangest thing happened. The crowd, seeing the girls approaching, magically parted, much as the waves of the Red Sea had parted for Moses and the Israelites.

Not knowing what to do next, the girls simply walked through the opening, up to the exhibit table. As they did, people started applauding and patting them on the back. "Nice job, girls!"

Now, *all* the girls were speechless. The crowd had been looking at their exhibit and apparently recognized them from the picture standing up in the framed newspaper article. Attached to their exhibit was the largest blue ribbon with gold lettering the girls had ever seen. It simply read: *Youth Category: Grand Champion.*

"Just when you think you've seen it all!" said Bryan.

The parents just stood there beaming. Before the girls could recover from the shock, several of the fairgoers started asking them all kinds of questions about their project and some even began taking pictures of the girls in front of their exhibit. Some even had their pictures taken with the girls, just by themselves.

The crowd never seemed to diminish. As some left, others would walk up. Several of Ava's classmates were there as well.

"You guys got Grand Champion!" her classmates said. "Way to go, Ava!"

"Well, I had help," Ava said, pointing to her sister and her two cousins. "You guys aren't mad at me, are you?"

"Heck no! It's about time someone else won that award!" one of the boys said.

Ava didn't know exactly what to say to that, so she just said, "Thanks."

As the question and answer session continued, Mr. Nelson made his way up to the table.

"Just stopped by to congratulate all of you on a job well done," he said. The girls thanked him for his support. "Don't thank me, you did all the work," he said. "Don't forget, when the fair is over next Saturday, you have that following week to pick up your exhibit." The girls looked at their parents and they all nodded.

The Dragonpillar

"And one more thing," Mr. Nelson added before leaving. "Although there is only one ribbon on your exhibit, I'm sure we can find a Grand Champion ribbon for each of you."

"Awesome!" they all exclaimed. "Thank you so much, Mr. Nelson!"

"And one last thing," he said. "I almost forgot. Since you won that award, your exhibit can be automatically entered in the State Fair later this summer, that is if you wish to participate. But we can talk about that later."

As Mr. Nelson left, the girls went back to answering questions from the crowd. Suddenly, Ava realized that all of her classmates had disappeared and the crowd was getting strangely quiet. She then noticed that everyone around her, for some reason, was staring behind her. She felt the hair on the back of her neck rise.

She slowly turned around to look, and there stood Mr. Holland. With his right hand extended out to her he said, "Congratulations, Ava. Your exhibit is excellent!"

Ava, completely caught off-guard, numbly shook his hand.

Stammering, Ava said. "Uh... thanks, Mr. Holland."

Recovering her composure somewhat, Ava said, "We honestly didn't know our exhibit was going to be judged, let alone be in the same category as our class project. We just thought Mr. Nelson asked us to put this together because of all the public interest, and for a couple of other reasons," she added, looking at her parents.

"That's all right," Mr. Holland said. Shaking the other three girls' hands, he said, "All of you girls worked very hard. I'm impressed with what you accomplished. You all deserve to be Grand Champions!"

Continuing, he added, "And your discovery! How exciting! I saw the picture in the paper and read the article when it came out."

Now looking back down the row of tables to where the class project sat, Ava said, "Well, I guess I now know why I got the 'A' in your science class."

"Yes," Mr. Holland said, "and now I understand why you kept the discovery of the 'Dragonpillars' a secret. Up until a few weeks ago, I didn't know about the 'CPR' thing, until your third grade teacher, Mr. Rocker, and I were discussing this year's class project and he filled me in on the details."

"Two years ago, when I took that butterfly off his desk, I honestly thought he had brought it in for me. I had no idea it was yours. Anyway, after Mr. Rocker explained to me how upset you were, I really didn't know what to say or do. As time went by, I just sort off pushed it to the back of my

167

mind. But this year, with you in my class, it all came back to me. I just decided to wait and see if you were able to find an insect to turn in. When the deadline passed, and you didn't turn anything in, well, it was easy for me to make the case that you simply turned your specimen in two years early."

The girls were still listening. No one knew just exactly to say at this point.

"Anyway," Mr. Holland said, "I'm glad I caught all of you here before we moved permanently. I just wanted to apologize for my mistake. I hope you can forgive me," he said to Ava.

"It's okay, Mr. Holland. I understand now," replied Ava. "It was an honest mistake. I really wasn't sure what had happened, but Mr. Rocker explained it to me after class that day, although at the time, all I could think about was my butterfly."

"Well," said Jill, changing the subject. "When are you moving?"

"Oh," replied Mr. Holland. "We've been moving furniture the past few weekends and will be totally out in two weeks. I've accepted another teaching position in Evansville."

"That's not too far, then," said Brett.

"No, it's not, and I have a new teaching tool for next year," he said, looking at the girls. "I have several copies of the newspaper that carried your story. First thing, when I get in my new classroom, I'm going to put a copy up on my bulletin board, so all of my students can see what might be possible if you just go out and try. It's just a great example of what you can accomplish with just hard work and a little ingenuity."

"And some luck," added Ellee. They all laughed.

"Thanks, Mr. Holland. That is awfully nice of you to say," Ava said.

"Ava," Mr. Holland said, "you were the hardest working student I had in all of my classes this year. I just want you to know that I didn't give you that 'A'. You earned that 'A'."

Mr. Holland, looking at his watch, now said he had to be going. As he shook everyone's hand again, the parents all said, "Good luck in your new position."

As he turned and made his way through the crowd, toward the entrance of the exhibit building, Ava yelled, "Mr. Holland, wait!"

Mr. Holland turned around and walked back up to the group. "Did I forget something?" he asked.

"No... uh... Mr. Holland," Ava said, looking down. "Before you go I want to apologize to you as well. I guess I listened to what some of the other kids were saying about you and I probably didn't give you a fair chance."

"Well," Mr. Holland said, patting Ava on the shoulder. "Don't worry about that, Ava. If I were in your shoes, I probably would have believed everything you heard too, especially after the 'butterfly' incident." He laughed.

"Oh, and next year, I'm going to take a different approach with my grading system. I think I may have put too much emphasis in the past on winning, but I've learned from you girls that winning is not the most important thing. It's really all about the effort you put in and how hard you work to get to the top that's important. And if any of my students next year have a GPA that is equivalent to an 'A', then all those students will get an 'A'," he said.

With the parents having just watched their daughters grow up a little right before their eyes, Brett said to Mr. Holland. "Hey, you know, we had a professional beekeeper get rid of those hornets up there in that shed. While you're still in town, why don't you drop by and we can go up there and see if we can find any antiques you'd like for your collection."

Surprised, Mr. Holland said, "Thanks, I just might do that."

Laughing, he said, "I did have a couple of tools in my hand that day, but I had to drop them when I had to run for my life!"

"Yeah, we remember!" the girls said, laughing. This time Brett and Bryan tried not to laugh, but were not very successful.

"Oh," Brett added, looking at Ava. "I think Ava might have something for you as well."

"Oh! That's right! I almost forgot!" she exclaimed.

"What is it?" asked Mr. Holland.

"Well, it's a surprise. You'll just have to come and see," Ava said, smiling.

"I'll do that," he said.

Mr. Holland turned and again made his way through the crowd. As he disappeared, Jill said to Brett, "That was really nice of you to offer that."

"Yeah, well, I'm the one supposed to be setting the example here, but today I had to take a lesson from my eleven-year-old daughter," he said, giving Ava a hug. Ava began to tear up again. The other three girls simply traded 'knuckles'.

"I wonder if he was always like that," Bryan mused, "or if he just had a change of heart."

At that moment, almost like magic, the answer popped into Ava's head. Pulling on her mother's arm, Jill bent down and Ava whispered something in her ear.

"I think you may be right, Ava, and I think that's a wonderful idea!" Jill whispered back. "We'll run it by your father when we get home."

After all that had just gone on in Exhibit Building No.4, the girls were ready to hit the midway. As they left the exhibit building, all the parents could hear was:

"I want a candy apple!"

"I want cotton candy!"

"I want a lemon shake-up!"

"I want to ride the Ferris wheel!"

The list of requests grew longer and louder the closer they got to the midway. As they approached the first ride, Ava asked, "Hey! Who's gonna ride on the Scrambler with me this year?"

The adults just looked at each other. All Ava heard from them was a resounding, "NO WAY!"

Chapter 38
The Conclusion

The summer had passed, and it was now a Saturday morning in mid-October. The girls had been back in school for two months, but were now on fall break. The weather was absolutely beautiful; low humidity, and not a cloud in the bright blue sky. Although it was a little cool, as the sun rose higher, the temperature was supposed to warm up quickly.

Everyone was sitting around the lake, trying to catch the large bass that were now feeding up in preparation for the long winter months ahead.

Ava was sitting with Snoop on an old blanket spread on the ground at her favorite fishing spot near the area where the mouth of the creek emptied into their lake. She knew, from catching fish there in the past, that this was a really good spot. The larger bass would wait in ambush for the minnows and smaller fish to be washed out of the creek into the lake.

Today she was using what her Uncle Bryan and her father called their 'secret' bait. It was an artificial minnow, about three inches long, made out of rubber. It mimicked the baitfish in the lake, and in the past, everyone using the 'secret' bait, had caught several large bass from time to time.

Ava wondered, "If everyone was using the 'secret' bait, could it really be that much of a secret!" No matter.

Papaw had driven up early that morning to check out the location Bryan and Lee Ann had picked out for their new house, but he also had brought his fishing pole along. From where she sat, Ava could see the stakes the contractors had driven in the ground, marking the lines where the foundation to their new house would be dug.

Looking around the lake, Ava could see Papaw, Uncle Bryan with Ellee and Isabelle, her father, and Brooklyn, all standing in different spots, all casting the 'secret' bait.

Brooklyn was standing close to Ava, keeping an eye on her success. As Ava would catch a bass and throw it back in, Brooklyn seemed to creep closer and closer to Ava. Ava didn't mind, but everyone else was laughing. The adults called that 'horning in' on someone else's good fishing spot.

Ellee had caught on to casting pretty quickly, but Bryan was getting an exercise in patience, trying to teach Isabelle how to fish. She kept getting her line tangled up in her father's line, in Ellee's line, or in the small trees behind her. So most of the time, that trio did not have their baits in the water. Bryan was displaying his usual good sense of humor, as even he was laughing at the wisecracks being made by all the 'professional' fishermen stationed around the lake.

"What are you catching over there, Bryan?" Brett yelled when Isabelle repeatedly got her line caught up in the trees behind her. "Tree bass?" Ava could hear everyone around the lake snickering.

"Looks like they're catching 'Stick-L-Backs' to me," said Papaw.

"It's much easier to catch fish if your bait is actually *in* the water," piped up Brooklyn.

Now Ava tried her hand at the wisecracks being directed Bryan's way. "I think they're catching 'Leaf Whoppers'," she yelled out.

"Leaf Whoppers! That's a good one, Ava," said Papaw. "I don't believe I've ever heard that one before."

"I just made that one up," Ava said proudly. Everyone was laughing now, even Isabelle.

"Not funny!" answered Bryan, now not appreciating the humor as much as he had earlier.

However, Ellee didn't get caught up in the fishing wisecracks. She had never caught the largest 'fish of the day', and was concentrating very hard today on doing just that. She had no time for the cheap comedy circulating around the lake. Nevertheless, so as not to hurt her sister's feelings, with each cast she made, she casually got further and further away from her sister.

By late morning, everyone had caught several small ones, but nothing really large. They all knew that there were bass in the lake weighing seven pounds and more, as they had caught and released several that size just last Spring.

As the sun climbed higher in the sky, though, the temperature started to warm up quickly. By eleven o'clock, it had become warmer than predicted, and the fish nearly stopped biting.

Getting hot, Ava decided to tie her hair back. Rummaging around in the top tray of her tackle box, she looked for a ribbon. Finding several wadded up in a ball, she saw her favorite color, pink. Pulling it out of the tangle, she paused, then laid it down. She pulled a purple one out.

The Dragonpillar

Tying her hair back with it, she said, "There, Snoop. This one matches my purple shirt. You want your hair tied back? I have a black one in here somewhere."

Hearing Ava talking to the dog, Ellee hollered across the lake. "Sorry, Snoop. No breadcrumbs today."

Snoop laid his head back down on his front paws, apparently disappointed that his aquatic skills would not be put on display this morning.

Jill was planning to fix hamburgers on the grill for lunch, so everyone had previously decided to fish till noon. With the fishing slowing down, Ava began reminiscing about everything that had happened since last spring.

Her first thought was of Isabelle. In late June they had Isabelle's 5th birthday party in the barn at the farmhouse. All the same family members attended, but this time it didn't rain and there was no crying. Isabelle's father bought her a pair of her very own official GI Joe binoculars, which she promptly took to Kindergarten the very first day for show and tell.

At the party, Brooklyn climbed the new ladder to the loft all by herself, although a railing *had* been installed. Isabelle now started squawking because her parents would not let her do it. *Maybe next year, Izzy.*

Now, thinking back to school herself, Ava found it hard to believe that a simple fifth grade science project had caused so much trouble, and then had set in motion a chain of events that had changed the lives of both families forever.

The weekend after the 4-H fair, Mr. Holland did indeed show up at the house before leaving town for good. Brett pulled the Gator out of the barn, once again hooked up the trailer, and took Mr. Holland up through the meadow to the shed. Ava and Brooklyn rode along in the backseat, and this time, even Snoop went along, sitting on the seat between the girls.

Reaching back to scratch Snoop's ears, Mr. Holland said, "Who says you can't teach an old dog new tricks?" They all laughed.

Whispering to Brooklyn, Ava said, "I know what Ellee would say if she were here."

"What's that?" Brooklyn asked, whispering back.

"A leopard *can* change its spots, get it?" Ava said, motioning to Mr. Holland.

Brooklyn just simply nodded her head. "I think you're right."

In the shed, Mr. Holland found a few tools he was interested in, even the ones he had dropped in a hurry to get away from the hornets. They piled them on the cart, and headed back.

When they got back to the farmhouse, Mr. Holland attempted to pay Brett for them, but he refused. "I think you've already paid enough," Brett said. The girls seemed to agree.

Mr. Holland thanked him, and Brett told him he could come back anytime he was in town.

"Thanks, I'll do that," he said.

As Mr. Holland started to get back in his truck, Ava remembered. "Wait!" she hollered. Ava ran into the house. Coming back out of the house, Ava handed Mr. Holland the shoebox.

"What's this?" he asked.

Ava just motioned for him to open it. Taking off the lid, he pulled out a pair of brown Italian loafers. "You didn't have to buy me a new pair of these!" he said to Ava in surprise.

"We didn't," said Ava. She let that sink in.

"Well... er... where did these come from?" Mr. Holland asked.

"Those are the shoes you lost in the pond," Ava said, smiling.

"How on earth did you get those back?" he asked again, totally astonished.

"You wouldn't believe me if I told you, right, Brooklyn?" Ava said.

Brooklyn just nodded her head.

Mr. Holland looked at Brett. Brett just shrugged his shoulders.

"Well, I don't know what to say but, thank you. You have all been so kind to me."

As Mr. Holland drove off, Ava smiled to herself. She was glad Mr. Holland would not be in town in two weeks for Halloween. They all yelled, "Come back and see us soon!"

Coming back to her senses, Ava decided it was time to check her bait. Reeling the artificial minnow in, she examined it, then cast the bait back out, just letting it float. Soon, she went back to daydreaming.

Several times that summer, Mr. Martin and his research team came back to the house, but the girls didn't go with them as often as before. One day in particular, they showed up with a few new faces. Two gentlemen, wearing suits and carrying briefcases, got out of their car. Rather than going over to the meadow, they spent most of the afternoon in the kitchen with their parents, and Uncle Bryan, and Aunt Lee Ann as well.

Cutting back and forth through the kitchen in an attempt to figure out what was going on, all the girls could see was a lot of paperwork spread out on the kitchen table.

On one trip through the kitchen, the girls saw their parents signing several documents. From the small talk around the table, they could tell their parents were extremely satisfied about something.

After the men left, it was some time before the girls found out what that meeting was all about. It wasn't until one afternoon in late July, when Bryan and Lee Ann met with a building contractor at the farmhouse, that the girls knew something was up.

As the building contractors began marking off the foundation for their new house, the girls could see that something had changed. Instead of building over in the meadow, they were apparently going to build just across the lake, no more than a couple of hundred yards from Ava and Brooklyn's back door. When the girls saw this, they began pumping their fists in the air and jumping for joy.

That's the day their parents told them what had happened.

The men in suits were from the state government. As the 'Dragonpillars' and the 'Pink Bobbys' had been declared 'endangered species', the state wanted to lease the meadow and turn it into a federally protected area. The lease would be for 99 years, with an option to renew the lease each time it expired.

"Wow! That's a long time!" Ava exclaimed.

In the lease agreement, it was agreed that the State would make monthly payments to both families for their 'loss of use' of the property for agreeing to set the land aside. Also, for the duration of the lease, the families would still own the ground, but would not have to pay property taxes on the leased acreage.

The parents told the girls this is what you call a 'win-win' for both parties involved.

In leasing the ground to the state, the area would be protected and forever remain in its natural state, thus making the scientific community happy. Also, their parents said a portion of the money being paid them by the State would be placed in a college fund being set up for each girl, since their parents could no longer divide up the meadow and sell off building lots as previously planned.

However, with this area now leased to the State and protected, that meant Bryan and Lee Ann could not build their new house over in the meadow. So the logical thing to do was to build it right across the lake, on Brett and Jill's seven acres.

While the attorneys were still at the house that day, Brett had them draw up paperwork, selling Bryan and Lee Ann the acreage they needed across the lake for their new house, for a grand total of one dollar. Now, when their house was finished, Ellee and Isabelle would only be shouting distance away.

"And," Brett said, "we're going to build a new bridge over the creek between the two houses, so you girls won't have to go over that old, rotten one anymore, and the new one will even be wide enough to drive the Gator over!"

"Awesome!" the girls all exclaimed.

The parents also told the girls that both families still retained the right to use the meadow as they saw fit, they just couldn't willfully damage or remove anything.

A few days after the meeting with the attorneys, Mr. Barry showed up with a couple of other conservation officers. All four girls were at the farmhouse, and Mr. Barry invited them to go with the men to help install signs around the meadow, declaring the property and everything in it protected by the federal government.

At the bottom of each sign, Ava read, "Maximum penalty for violations: $10,000 per person, per violation."

"That ought to keep people out!" Brooklyn said.

"Leaving the bull up here probably would have been more effective," said Ellee.

The Dragonpillar

The conservation officers broke out into laughter. "Ellee," laughed Mr. Barry, "I think you might have a good point there. By the way, where did you learn to talk like that?"

Ellee, handing everyone bottles of partially frozen water from her backpack, just shrugged her shoulders.

Ava now laughed to herself, remembering one of the last sleepovers they had at the farmhouse, right before school started up again, last August.

That night, Ava, thinking everyone had gone to sleep, heard Brooklyn climb down from the top bunk. Quietly going across the room, she heard Brooklyn open up one of her dresser drawers. After a long pause, she heard the drawer quietly being shut. Brooklyn climbed back up the ladder, not knowing Ava was still awake.

The next morning, after Brooklyn, Ellee, and Isabelle had gone downstairs to eat breakfast, Ava slid out of bed and went over to Brooklyn's dresser. Opening the bottom drawer, she saw 'Bobby' neatly folded and tucked away. Ava never asked her sister about it or brought up the subject again. Apparently the 'Bobby' era was over.

However, the next night, when all four girls were again getting ready for bed, Ellee said, "Anyone seen my Bobby?"

"Yeah!" wailed Isabelle, "My Bobby's missing too!"

"They're in the dryer," Jill yelled up the stairs.

Apparently the Bobby era was not over, Ava realized, laughing to herself.

Just then, Snoop growled, startling Ava. The geese walking around the lake were apparently getting to close for his comfort.

"Get'em, Snoop!" Ava said, now back in the moment at hand.

Just then, an awful racket erupted from the direction of the barn. Ava figured it was more of the geese. Looking to her left, however, she saw that it was just several chickens chasing each other around the barn, squawking and apparently fighting over something, or maybe fighting over nothing at all, as the chickens often seemed to do.

"Hey! The barn!" Ava said to herself.

At that moment she realized they had all been so busy the past few months, they had forgotten all about the 'big secret' her father and Uncle Bryan had been working on in the barn last summer.

Looking around the lake, Ava thought to herself that after the adults have stuffed themselves with burgers and fries and are taking a nap, she would get the girls together and do a little more exploring.

Studying the barn a little more closely, Ava caught sight of the sign that had been erected along the creek where it ran behind the barn, emptying into the lake, near the spot where she was now fishing. She smiled to herself.

She remembered that day during the fair, in the exhibit building, when she had whispered something to her mother as Mr. Holland was leaving. Once they got home from the fair, Jill ran Ava's idea by her father. He immediately went into the barn. About an hour later, after some sawing and painting, he emerged with the sign.

Brett, Jill, Ava, Brooklyn, with Snoop in tow, took the sign down to the creek and conducted a small ceremony before Brett drove the stake, with the attached sign, into the ground near the edge of the water, officially christening the stream.

Now, looking at the sign, Ava could easily read the bright yellow letters her father had carved and painted, proclaiming the revelation that had come to her at the precise moment her Uncle Bryan had posed the question about Mr. Holland's apparent change of heart.

The sign simply read: Little River Jordan.

At that moment, Ava felt the slightest tug on her line and sensed movement, as the tip of her fishing pole bent slightly down. She was immediately brought back to the task at hand. She was sure a fish had taken up her bait, but when she re-focused on what she was doing, she saw it was not a fish at all. Rather it was a strange looking insect, with bright pink dots running along its sides, sitting on the tip of her fishing rod.

"Hey!" Ava exclaimed. "What are you doing here? I thought you would be hibernating in your cave by now."

Ava held out her arm and the insect immediately flew down, landing on the palm of her hand. The insect blinked its eyes and fanned its wings, which tickled Ava's hand. However, Ava didn't laugh this time.

"You will always be my friend. I will never forget you," she said, the tears welling up in her eyes.

The Dragonpillar

Although Ava knew the 'Dragonpillar' couldn't actually speak, she knew the insect was here to tell her goodbye. To Ava's surprise, the insect flew down and landed on her open tackle box. It crawled around, apparently examining its contents.

At that moment, Ava heard the screen door on the back 'deck-porch' slam shut, open, then slam shut again. Jill yelled, "Burgers are ready!"

Ava turned to see her mother shoveling burgers off the grill onto a large plate. When she turned back around, the Dragonpillar was gone. Thinking it might have crawled inside her tackle box, she checked, but it wasn't there. It had flown away.

Looking around the lake, Ava could see that everyone had begun stowing their fishing gear, and were now all heading back to the house for lunch. Ava reeled in her line and began putting her tackle box back in order.

However, Ava noticed something seemed to be missing. She looked around on the ground, but didn't see it. She looked under the blanket she was sitting on. It wasn't there either. She then went through the contents of her tackle box with the same result.

All of a sudden, she realized where it was.

She looked to the north, past the barn and up through the meadow, to the wooded hills. Ava knew then, that this winter, at least one Dragonpillar would be sleeping in a nest lined with a pink ribbon.

Turning back around to the house, Ava said, "Come on, Snoop. Let's go get some lunch."

The End

About the Author

The author lives with his wife in Seymour, Indiana. He is a retired parks and recreation administrator and also a retired professional firefighter. He now owns and manages a small construction business, enjoys hunting, fishing, reading, writing, and still plays travel softball with a team located out of Indianapolis. He and his wife enjoy spending as much time as possible with their two sons and daughters-in law, and of course their four granddaughters.

If you would like to contact the author, you can email him at: robertsonarthur@hotmail.com. But a word of caution. He only checks his email account once a week at best. However, he would still love to hear what your thoughts are on his first book.

Acknowledgements

No book is the work of a single individual, so I am told, and so it was with the completion of this book.

At this time I would like to thank the many people who helped and guided me through the process of finishing this book and getting it published.

First of all I would like to thank two retired high school teachers from my hometown, who I turned to for assistance early on: Mr. Brantley Blythe and Mr. Jon Geuder.

As it had nearly been forty years since I had last sat in an English class, my spelling, punctuation, and grammar were atrocious, to say the least. I gave the first draft of my story to Mr. Blythe, a retired high school English teacher, and he graciously went through my two hundred and thirty, scribbled, handwritten pages, correcting my many mistakes. I am indebted to him for his patience and willingness in doing this for me.

Secondly, I would also like to thank Mr. Jon Geuder, also a retired high school English and Spanish teacher who, (I am almost ashamed to admit this), loaned me a functioning laptop, with which I could work on my story. When I picked up the laptop, he also gave me a quick lesson on its operation and features, as my computer skills were also somewhat rusty at that time. Without his assistance, the story would still be lying in my basement collecting dust.

Next, I would be remiss if I didn't thank the people involved with the 'Spilling Ink Writers Group' who meet once a month at our local library. I had no idea this group existed, until I drove by the library one day and saw an announcement for an upcoming meeting on their message board. I attended the meeting and learned that the group consisted of several individuals who have already written and published several books. They graciously provided me with guidance and assistance with regards to the publishing process, and I am indebted to them for their patience and understanding with my never-ending list of questions. I would like to specifically thank the group leader, Kathi Linz, Information Services Assistant at the library and her husband Les, both established authors in their own right, who provided me with invaluable information regarding this whole process.

I would also like to thank another group member, Emma (Shade) VonDielingen, an author in her own right as well, who I leaned on the most. She cheerfully answered my never-ending list of questions about this process and assisted me in formatting my book and getting it sent in for e-book publication.

I would also like to thank my illustrator, Darnell Dukes, chief administrator of the Southern Indiana Center for the Arts, who designed the cover for my book. She is an exceptional artist in her own right, and her beautiful artwork bought the story to life. I am indebted to her for her contribution to the book.

Next I would like thank Sommer Stein, who designed the jacket for my book. She did a beautiful job as well and also provided me with invaluable suggestions about this process.

Finally I would like to thank C.J. Pinard who conducted the final copyedit on my manuscript. Her efforts in correcting my remaining mistakes and her constructive criticism concerning content in a few areas (lol) of the story were invaluable. She is a true professional and I am honored that she took the time to help out a 'rookie'.

Without her and all the individuals listed above, the completion of this book would not have been possible.